Nobody Goes Out Anymore

NOBODY GOES OUT ANYMORE
By D.L. Russell

Edited by D. L. Russell
Copy/Line Editing by Joanna Hoyt

ISBN: 9798669930660

DLR
Indiana, U.S.A.

Published by D. L. Russell

DEDICATION

This anthology is dedicated to **Mary Patterson-Thornburg** because except for my mother, Mary has been the most intense source of encouragement and mentorship in my life. She has been around since my Strange, Weird, and Wonderful Magazine days, and without her motivation, I'm not sure if I would have ever had the confidence to publish a book.

Thank You Mary!

CONTENTS

FOREWORD

Stephen King says the question he hears most often is, "Where do you get your ideas?" That may be the question every writer hears most often. My favorite answer to it is one I heard from science-fiction writer Charles Coleman Finlay: he said he has them shipped in by the gross, wholesale, from China. But the truth is, writers get ideas wherever they can find them - beg, borrow, or flat-out steal. Sometimes ideas come from dreams, or from a story someone's grandmother told them. Often, they come from things happening in the writer's world - things good or not-so-good.

In the 1300's, in Italy, a writer named Giovanni Boccaccio wrote a whole collection of love stories about a group of ten young men and women hiding out together, trying to escape the Great Bubonic Plague - what we sometimes call the Black Death. That was a bad one, thought to have wiped out up to sixty percent of Europe's population, and some of Boccaccio's stories are sad. But some are funny, and some are very erotic. The events of history touch storytellers and their stories in different ways, sometimes directly and sometimes indirectly. During a plague time, a time of sheltering in place, people live with their memories and their imaginings.

As the stories in this book were being written, and as the book is being published, we are living in a plague time. This time will change and it will pass, one way or another. Our present will become someone else's past. These stories will survive. And, as they may help us now to think about our own time and its possible future(s), they will tell people in that future - or one of those possible futures - something about how these sixteen writers were thinking and feeling here and now, in the thick of things.

Mary Patterson Thornburg
7/29/2020

INTRODUCTION

The Coronavirus (severe acute respiratory syndrome coronavirus 2) went from a side-note most people in the United States believed only concerned China to a full blown hot mess in a matter of months. Large numbers of people were really dying and health officials from around the world were sounding the alarm. insisting this was not like the "Illness Scares," of the past few decades. This wasn't H1N1, this wasn't Ebola, this wasn't MERS, and this wasn't the Zika Virus. This was different, and this was going to be BAD!

Schools closed, professional sports leagues canceled their seasons, businesses were ordered to shut down, and everyone else was told to Shelter-In-Place.

As I write this in the beginning of the 2nd half of 2020, there is still no end in sight to the pandemic. World governments don't know what to do and their citizens are becoming more and more divided and fearful of where we go from here.

Honestly, the stories in this anthology are not where we want to be, but the hand we're playing ain't all that promising, and to quote the most despicable phrase of the 21st century, "it is…what it is."

DLR
7/27/2020

UNDER THE SHADOW

Joanna Michal Hoyt

When the Sequel virus first appeared in the news, here in Beulahsville our main concern was how it would affect the race for mayor. Eleanor Drehle had beaten Ed Grant last time by 927 votes to his 709. The second campaign was louder and angrier than the first - partly because Eleanor was blocking Ed's latest fly-by-night business idea and partly because everyone just was angrier by then - and it tore up whatever was left of our unity as the miracle village.

Two years before, when COVID-19 was burning through the country and the news was full of body bags and system collapses, no one from Beulahsville died of the virus, or was hospitalized for it, or was diagnosed with it - or tested for it, either; the nearest hospital was an hour away in Stonebrook, and they were busy dealing with the people who were at death's door.

We stayed put in Beulahsville. The farmers kept farming. Folks who worked in schools or factories in bigger towns stayed home because the schools and the factories closed. Our kids (what few we had) stopped busing out to school for the same reason. Marlis and Will and Janie worked away at stores that stayed open, but pretty soon they were staying in the stores overnight too, taking turns watching for burglars. Most of us were "too old to work and too young to die," and we sewed masks with fabric from Ev's dollar store and sent boxes of them away to stricken places. We sent care packages to Marlis and Will and Janie too, until the postal service shut down. Then we hunkered down and waited. And we were spared. We were all spared.

Eleanor said, afterward, that we'd been spared because we'd kept to ourselves. Reverend Ellis at Grace Chapel (where Ed goes) said we'd been spared because his parishioners had prayed with faith. Pastor Eunice at Beulahsville Unity Church (where Eleanor goes) said that was an insult to the faithful people who'd died of the virus elsewhere, and that faith didn't guarantee health. Reverend Ellis said that was an insult to the power of the Lord. They didn't speak to each other for weeks. Some folks from their congregations said things to each other that would've been better unsaid.

That's how it was all over the country, if you believe the news. After the dying was done the Democrats and the Republicans blamed each other for the damage, took credit for what was salvaged, and said that the disaster showed that it was time for major reforms. They couldn't agree on what the reforms should be, so things went on as before, only with no public postal service, and precious little health insurance for anyone who wasn't rich, and most people poorer, and everyone angry and afraid. It's a wonder more people didn't get killed around the election. We had some of that anger in Beulahsville, but we weren't so frightened, seeing as we'd been spared by our prudence or our faith.

Or by our healthy location, up on the high plateau in the wind and the sun and away from the cities with all their sicknesses and foreigners. That was Ed's theory. He said we ought to share our blessings prudently and capitalize on them. He meant to do that by cutting the farmland he'd inherited from his uncle Elmer (which had been in dairy until the milk prices collapsed, and under weeds and brush since then) into house lots and selling it to "desirable residents." Seemingly that meant "rich people," given the prices he thought to charge. I wasn't the only one who laughed and said no "desirable residents" would want to come out to a dying town in the sticks.

Yes, the town was dying, though we'd all survived the pandemic. The car plant in Stonebrook never reopened, and lots of folks who'd worked there moved away from Beulahsville to seek work. A few, like Hollis up the road, stayed home and took up subsistence farming and hunting full-time. So there was even less money floating round town than there'd been before the pandemic, and Jim's bar/diner shut down.

Then all we had left for business was Ev's dollar store, and Brent and Avis' gas station, and Rusty's weekly runs to towns big enough to have a for-pay mail delivery service.

Ed said once rich people came the town would revive, and he said he had customers biting. Well, Ed always said his businesses were raring to go, until they failed. But when some developer in a flashy suit and a flashier car visited Ed, Eleanor reckoned it was serious. She told Ed the land wasn't zoned for subdivision and he'd have to ask for a variance from the zoning board.

The mayor, by law, was one of the three members of the zoning board. The other two members were separately elected in off years. Those were Jim, who was all for Ed's idea, and Hollis, who was dead set against it. Ed couldn't go ahead without getting elected mayor. Eleanor said she wanted to keep Beulahsville the way it had always been and keep it safe the way she had during the pandemic. Ed said the pandemic was done but poverty would kill the town if Eleanor and Hollis kept fighting yesterday's battles.

So when news reports mentioned a mutation of the virus —the Sequel, they called it, since it spun off from the novel coronavirus- was coming back in some cities far from us, with a death rate even higher than the last time, Eleanor's backers said she'd saved us once and would save us again, while Ed would kill us all off for quick cash. Some of Ed's supporters said the mutated virus was fake news. After the TV ran footage of piled body bags, Ed's backers allowed the disease was real, but said it was just in those filthy cities full of foreigners and that wasn't who Ed was asking... You can imagine how it went from there.

People argued, not just about the Sequel itself, but about the craziness that seemed to be spreading alongside it: the Shadow, some people called that. Oh, there were still heartwarming stories about folks bringing food for shut-ins, about hospitals treating uninsured patients for free. But there were more stories about murder and suicide rates going up even faster than the contagion rates in stricken cities. In one city an angry crowd burned down the free hospital. Grace Chapel and Beulahsville Unity Church both asked for prayers for the afflicted and took up collections for the hospitals. Reverend Ellis preached on "Touch not the unclean thing" and "The wages of sin is death," and he said that sin was as deadly as any virus and that maybe the city folks' sin had laid them open to sickness. Pastor Eunice said it was fear made people do most of the harm we did, and she preached on "Be not afraid" and "Perfect love drives out all fear." She looked terrified. Most of us didn't rightly see why she should be afraid; the cities were having emergencies, sure, but the governor hadn't declared an emergency, nor the president, and the closest cases were hours away in places where we never went, and anyway we'd been spared before when everyone else was stricken.

Then our county health department said that there was a case of the Sequel in the county.

Loads of us called them to ask where. Most of the phone-answerers stonewalled, but someone gave actual information to three of Eleanor's backers and two of

Ed's. They all got the same word: The case was in Beulahsville.

We weren't special, weren't spared. One of us was sick. One of us was a danger to everybody else. The Health Department wouldn't say who it was.

Folks on the Beulahsville social media page—no, not the official one, the one where the real conversations happen—agreed on that. That was all they agreed on.

Avis: *It's Ed. Got to be. That city rat snuffling around his property must have given it to him.*

Janie@Avis: *Or to anyone else he glad-handed.*

Sara@Avis: *Why pick on Ed and his visitor? Plenty of people leave town for work...*

Will@Sara: *This isn't like last time. The sickness wasn't anywhere near us. Someone from way away must have brought it.*

Sally@Will: *You know who else we've had here from way away? That alien that gave the program at the Unity Church three weeks ago, after they'd already started reporting on the Sequel in the cities.*

Avis@Sally: *Idiot, the mission speaker wasn't from a city, nor from a galaxy far far away.*

Hollis@Avis: *I told you as soon as the news broke: we needed to stock up and stay home. That's what I did. It's not me risking everyone's life. Till I know which of you it is, I'll be sheltering in place. Keep off my property.*

Jim@Hollis: *No one's going to miss you, except your lapdog Eleanor. Maybe she can join you.*

Hollis@Jim: *Speaking of dogs, you...*

It went downhill from there, fast. I told myself to log off that site, but somehow, I couldn't. There was a high shrill ringing in my ears like what they say old factory workers get, but I'd worked in the school (way back when Beulahsville had one) not on the line. The hotter the argument got on the screen, the louder that ringing got, and the less I felt able to look away.

Angie Kreutzer's post paused the conversation.

Angie: *You ablative cretins! Aunt Mabel has the Sequel. The home health aide came with a test kit. Now I'm shut in with Aunt Mabel and I can't keep a nidificating social distance because somebody has to change the sheets and that has to be me because the health aide won't touch her again. Didn't touch her on the last visit—handed the test to me and did some digital stuff and said the test was positive. Wouldn't test me because the test doesn't work until the symptoms start, though the virus is contagious before then. Told me I can't leave the house. I'm bloody sitting*

> *here waiting to get sick and die and I log on to ask can anyone leave supplies on the porch and I see this absquatulating dogpile about the infarcted election and all your verecund feuds!*

Angie doesn't let herself swear, but she's got the Kreutzer temper, and she fills in the blanks with Increase Your Word Power vocabulary. Well, this time she had cause to be angry. I tried to call her. Got a busy signal.

Ten minutes later Angie posted that she'd been offered more food than she and Mabel could eat in a month of Sundays, and she was grateful, but now would people please stop calling because she had a headache.

Headache, we all knew by then, was one of the early symptoms of the Sequel.

Eleanor posted to congratulate us on our solidarity, but she forbade us to go onto Mabel's property and maybe get infected. She said food should be dropped at the end of the driveway, without the driver stepping out of the car.

Avis said that was fine in good weather and while Angie was still able to go in and out easily, but on rainy days the food would get ruined, and if Angie...

Angie's next post, *DO YOU MIND NOT TALKING ABOUT ME DYING WHERE I CAN SEE IT?* didn't stop people arguing about whether the Sequel could be spread on shoe soles, on tire treads... Nor did it stop the side thread about how Mabel could have gotten it before anyone else, since she'd not been able to leave her house for eighteen months. Folks from both churches visited her, of course, and Angie looked after her, but...

Jim wrote that he'd looked across the street and seen the home health worker fill her car with gas at the pump. He didn't know if that had been before or after she was in Mabel's house.

Maybe it doesn't matter, Ed wrote. *Maybe she gave it to Mabel. You can tell she's not from around here. Who knows where she's been? And now she's contaminated the gas station.*

She's from Stonebrook, Avis answered. *She told me last week she'd been there twenty years. And why you should blame her...*

You were talking to her? That was Jim again. *Last week? The Sequel can take three weeks to show up. Don't come near me! Don't go to Ev's store, either! Or anyplace else we have to be!*

You didn't see Solange filling her car up from your window, Avis replied. *You were in line after her at the gas pump. So don't go lecturing as if you were clean and safe.*

You're all crazy, Hollis posted*, and maybe you're all sick. If any of you come on my land, I'll shoot.*

Avis went offline then. So did Eleanor and Ed. I turned away from my computer and looked out the window.

I live on the main road, between Mabel's house and the gas station, though closer to Mabel's. I watched Avis' beat-up blue Ford roll by toward Mabel's house. Food drop, I figured, before Eleanor got in there with her sanitary protocols.

Eleanor drove after Avis, laying on the horn. Sanitary protocols, I figured.

Then came Ed's black pickup truck. I didn't know what he thought he was doing.

First I thought the ringing in my ears was getting louder. Then I realized it was the telephone.

It was Brent, Avis' husband. His voice was shrill. "Did Avis go by your house?"

"Yes, she..."

"And Ed chasing her?"

"I don't know about *chasing*. He was behind Eleanor..."

"Mike said Ed loaded his rifle into his pickup truck. It's not hunting season."

"Calm down," I said. "Ed may be a jerk, but he's not a murderer. He and Avis have had spats before, and..."

"What if he's got the Shadow now?"

"Brent, take a deep breath," I said. "Ed's not going to shoot Avis."

"Not if I get there in time," Brent said, and he hung up.

The ringing in my ears was so loud it made my head ache. I hoped that was why my head was aching. I hoped it wasn't the Sequel. I didn't have time to worry about that; I had my neighbors to worry about. I hurried out the front door and down the sidewalk toward Mabel's house.

Avis' car was pulled up by the end of Mabel's driveway, and Eleanor's car was parked right behind it. Avis and Eleanor stood halfway up Mabel's driveway, each holding one handle of Avis' cooler, tugging it different ways and yelling at each other. I thought I caught "inhumane" from Avis and "reckless endangerment" from Eleanor. Behind their cars Ed's truck was slewed around crossways, blocking both lanes. Ed wasn't in the truck. Ed stood in the middle of the road in front of their cars, holding his rifle pointed at the pavement.

"Mayor Drehle, our sanitary savior," Ed yelled. "You're already in the contamination zone. You can't come back out and make us all sick now. You said so yourself. Get in that house, both of you, and don't come out!" The women dropped the cooler and yelled Ed's name in identical tones of exasperation, starting back down the driveway toward him.

He pointed the rifle at Eleanor. "Stop," he said.

I'd had Ed in my sixth-grade class thirty-odd years before, in the last year we had our own school in Beulahsville. I called his cocky eleven-year-old face to mind. "Edward Timothy Grant, Junior," I said in my teacher voice, "put that down right now." I started toward him.

"Stop, Miss Czernicki!" Brent wailed behind me.

"He won't shoot me," I said.

"He won't shoot anyone. I'll get him first. But..."

"Don't you dare!" That was Sally's voice—where had she come from? "Brent, I'm recording you, and if you..."

"Ed started this," Eleanor said. "He's the one someone should be recording...."

"I am." That was Ev's voice.

"He's criminal, insane, or both," Eleanor said. "Clearly not fit to be Mayor."

Ed made an ugly little sound in his throat. I stepped toward him, calling his name again.

"Don't get any closer, Miss Czernicki!" Brent said, and his voice sounded strange, though it might just have been the ringing in my ears. "He's got the Shadow! Don't get close enough so he can give it to you!" Brent's face looked as wrong as his voice sounded.

"You sure he hasn't given it to you already?" My voice, asking that, sounded wrong too. Terribly wrong. My head hurt. My head...

Inspiration, or desperation, struck. I folded up in the middle of the lane and fake-coughed loudly and dramatically into both hands, shaking violently for good measure. I sat down before I could fall down with the shaking, and I kept on coughing.

The yelling stopped. All I heard was the ringing in my ears and a couple more of my own fake coughs. Then a small, worried voice: "Miss Czernicki, are you all right?" That was Ed, and he sounded the way he had when he was a boy and I found him bent over a bird with a broken wing - not tormenting it, but trying clumsily to set its wing, and crying.

I opened my mouth to say something reassuring. Instead I coughed. Involuntarily, this time. I kept coughing until my chest hurt. I coughed into my hands and kept my head down between my knees, but I doubted that was enough to keep me from contaminating my neighbors.

"Nobody's all right," I gasped. "Get out, all of you. Go home."

"You need help," Ed insisted.

"Call 911," Ev said.

"It wouldn't help." Eleanor's voice was flat. "I've been following the news on that. They're not sending crews out for potential Sequel patients. Not after last time. And Stonebrook won't take Sequel patients even if they're driven there, even if they can pay."

Well, Stonebrook had lost half its doctors, and more than half its nurses and its cleaning staff, in the pandemic or the aftermath. And they, like most other hospitals, had been hard put to it to hire more, before the Provider Discretion Act... well, to tell the truth I'd not bothered my mind much with the details, but I guessed the Act let them turn people like me away.

"The hell they won't!" Brent said. "What's she supposed to do? She can't go home like this - she can't go home alone, and we can't go in."

"She can join us," Angie called from her window. "I'll call Solange and tell her to add to the emergency kit she's sending us tomorrow."

"Miss Czernicki might not have Sequel," Ed objected. "You might make her sick."

"She might have the Shadow," Brent objected. "She might hurt you."

"We might all have everything," Eleanor said, sounding dead. Then she shook herself and spoke in her mayor voice again. "For now, go home, and don't touch anyone or go into any other buildings. I'll contact the Health Department. We'll.... we'll get through this somehow. I hope. As for the Shadow, I suppose the best thing we can do is remember not to kill each other, or anyone else."

I went into another coughing fit.

"Get out, all of you, so I can get Miss Czernicki in!" Angie hollered. They obeyed.

***

That was three nights ago. Mabel's buried in the back yard. Angie did that, since I vomited when I tried to stand up. Angie's not doing so badly; her head hurts, but that could be stress, and her eyes hurt, but that could be crying about Mabel. She's still eating the food that someone rolled to our door in a kid's wagon with a note saying to unpack the wagon and shove it back down the drive and let it sit out in the sun for a week till the germs died. I think the handwriting on the note was Ev's, and she maybe donated the store-bought stuff, but Sally's pickles and Pastor Eunice's gingersnaps and Jim's homemade wine were in the wagon too, and so was a vase of flowering branches from the ornamental crabs in front of Grace Chapel's rectory. Eleanor and Ed both sent me and Angie kind emails. They're both sick and have shut themselves in. So have Avis and Brent.

So, also, is Hollis. Seemingly the Sequel was among us before any of us knew it. Likely we'll never know how it came, and I don't expect to live to see how it goes. The Shadow, though—I think that's always been with us, waiting to break out, spreading fast when it does. I suppose at Grace Chapel they'd call it sin, and at Beulahsville Unity they'd call it fear. Whatever it may be, we're fighting it off as well as anybody can. And maybe those of us who live through the Sequel – I think some of us might – will be immune to the Shadow if it comes back around.

EARNESTINE GREEVES, YOU DONE FUCKED UP...

D.L. Russell

March 17th, 2021

When they found her, Earnestine Medusa Greeves could hardly breathe. The coronavirus had taken hold in her 83-year-old lungs and seemed determined to take her life. Her death, twenty-four hours later, made national news…

March 1st, 2021

"Thank you, Ja'Quan," Earnestine said to the young man from the house on the other side of Airborne

Street. He'd just helped carry her meager groceries into her old Victorian after giving her a ride to the grocery store, whose shelves always seemed to be just as meager during this time of worldwide crisis.

The seven-bedroom Second Empire was three times as old as Earnestine and, since the death of her husband Ralph Reeves, hadn't had more than a handful of people enter through its weathered doors with their peeling paint and rusted hinges. But the house, although in need of repair, thrived with life.

"I see you got another one," Ja'Quan said as he turned at the step, referring to a dark gray kitten hunkered under Mrs. Greeves' rose bushes. "He looks sick, though."

Earnestine didn't pay no mind to Ja'Quan after he'd pointed out the tiny darling under the bush. She stepped onto the porch to get a closer look, and, as her heart swelled for the poor little thing, she couldn't help but go pick it up and hold it close to her sagging, defeated bosom.

"Oh, you poor little thing," she found herself saying, taking the kitten into her house, kissing its forehead, and nuzzling its whiskers. She put the kitten down and her matriarch cat walked over to check out the new visitor.

"Yes, I do believe we've found number fifteen," Earnestine said to Perilya. "Let's make him feel at home."

Perilya released a somewhat bland meow, walked up to the kitten for a perfunctory sniff, and immediately decided the thing needed to die. With the speed of her ancient ancestors the twenty-year-old tabby hissed and began to deliver a series of claw-extended jabs, crosses, and uppercuts to the new visitor.

"Perilya!" Earnestine shouted, borrowing a little speed from her own ancestors to kick the tabby halfway across the front room.

Perilya made no other attempts to attack, but instead ran off into the bowels of the house, hollering as if the sky was falling.

"Emergency meeting! Emergency meeting!" Perilya shouted as she ran up the stairs. "Emergency meeting! The Human has let death into the building! Death is in the building!"

"What's going on, Ya?" Simon asked calmly. He was one of the few cats who had been trained to use and flush the toilet, and he had just finished his business in the cat-bathroom.

"What's got you so bothered, Mom?" This time it was Julia, who had also just finished up in the cat-bathroom, though, unlike Simon, she'd simply gone in the litter-filled bathtub.

By now almost all the other cats had come out into the hallway, curious as to what was happening.

"The Human, in her ignorance," Perilya began to explain, panting from her effort, "has a new young one down there, and I smelled death on it!"

"Are you sure?" That was Brutus, coming out of Cat-Room Number One at the end of the hall. As the dominant male of the house, he had been lounging with several of the younger females. A long time ago he and Perilya had been lovers, but now, not so much.

Brutus, a big Maine Coon, had spent most of his sixteen years as an alley cat. Earnestine had taken him in from a shelter after a group of juvenile delinquents had been caught trying to literally skin him alive.

"Yes, I'm sure, Brutus!" Perilya hissed. "I know the smell of death!"

"I believe you, Mother," Erma, the white ragamuffin, told her. "I've never seen you this upset."

Several of the other cats expressed their agreement. Perilya was not one to panic, and she never lied to them.

"Go see for yourself!" Perilya insisted.

"I'll have a look with you, Brut," Simon said.

"No! I'll go by myself." Brutus glared at Simon, his expression giving away his displeasure. In the male hierarchy of the building, Simon wasn't old enough to speak on important situations unless he was being questioned by an elder.

In the twelve months since the governor had put Indiana on lockdown from the coronavirus pandemic, Earnestine hadn't needed to alter her life as much as others. Being a somewhat wealthy widow with a love of cats and of ordering items from QVC and Amazon, she had been living in an unrealized quarantine for years.

If there were items she couldn't have delivered, she would slip a twenty to Ja'Quan or his wife, and they would either run to pick it up for her, or drive her where she needed to go.

Earnestine was surprised none of the other felines had come down to take a look at the newest member of their clan, who had refused to eat or even sip milk from a saucer, so far. She loved her cats, even if Perilya could be a fussy little bitch sometimes, she thought while rocking and cooing to the kitten and looking at the twelve o'clock news.

According to WANE-TV, people were still dying, new cases were being reported every day, and unfortunately the virus had began to mutate from its original strain into a version able to kill you in half the time.

Earnestine didn't fear death, but she wasn't ready to start picking out a casket either. She had her cats and her mind still, and although she did sometimes want for the touch of a man, she felt blessed for having all she needed. This included the three pistols and the shotgun she kept stashed around the house just in case that damned virus started turning everyone into looters or maybe even zombies. She knew she could never seriously harm a cat, but people, now that was a different story.

***

Perilya rested at the bend in the stairs, waiting for Brutus to finish up downstairs. She had wanted to go with him, but he'd insisted she stay and make sure no one else went down.

"You were right," Brutus said flatly, towering over her suddenly. She hated how he could scare her. "But there's no need to worry anymore. The thing is dead now."

"Brutus, you killed it! That's awesome. I tried to take care of it then and there, but the Human gave me her foot. That's when I ran up the stairs in a panic!"

"No, no, no!" Brutus shouted. "Nothing like that at all."

"Oh... Oh, so what happened?"

"If you could just shut your gray-whiskered lips for a moment, I'll tell you!"

"Well, spit it out! Everyone else is up there napping in one place or another. It's just you and I awake."

"I went down there," Brutus began, as he walked a full circle around Perilya before flopping down on the step above her, "as quietly as possible, of course, and the Human had the kitten in her lap."

"Our Human can really be stupid sometimes," Perilya interrupted. "You know, I was telling Simon once…"

"Let me finish!" Brutus insisted while flopping her across the head with his heavy tail.

"Okay. Finish up."

"As I said, I saw the two of them in the chair the male Human used to sit in before he fell down the stairs and died, but the chair wasn't moving like it usually does. Then I realized the female Human was asleep. I could tell because that dreadful noise was coming from her face."

"Oh I hate when she does that."

"Can I finish?"

"Yes, Brutus," Perilya answered, with a hint of laughter in her purring."

"You're not funny," he told her, but also delivered a more lingering, playful swipe of his tail.

"Go on, Brutus," she insisted softly.

"Anyway, as I crept closer I realized the little thing wasn't asleep, but watching my approach. And, as you said, I could smell death on him as strong as anything.

""Help me," he said, as I stopped close enough to him to get a solid sniff. At that point I felt somewhat sorry for him. I hadn't expected that."

"What can I do, little one?" I asked.

""Stay with me as I die," he barely got out, and then he reached out a tiny paw and I extended mine to him."

"Did you wake the Human?" Perilya interrupted again.

"No, no. I was being very gentle. The Human just kept on making that noise, but before I knew what happened the kitten sneezed on me."

"Sneezed on you?" This new bit of information caused Perilya to rise up on her front legs.

"Yes, so I had to jump back and clear the moisture from my face and whiskers, and when I looked at him again, his head had rolled to one side. His eyes were open, but I knew he was no longer there."

For the first time that day, Perilya was speechless.

After the death of the kitten, Earnestine buried him in the plot in her backyard where she put all the cats that passed away while living with her. She hadn't bothered to identify each individual grave but had placed a simple hand-painted marker at the furthest corner of the space.

Within days the house seemed to return to normal, and the cats roamed around in their uninhibited fashion, mostly upstairs, but on occasion stopping downstairs just to see how their Human was faring. Most realized it wasn't normal for any creature to be alone so much, but Perilya had explained to them how they were her family now since her mate, the male Human, had fallen down the stairs and died.

Two full weeks passed before anyone, cat or human, began to realize anything was wrong.

For Earnestine, it was waking with an urge to go to the bathroom because of loose bowels. She couldn't remember the last time she had needed to take anything for diarrhea, or constipation for that matter. Her old pipes were pretty regular but considering she had consumed a healthy portion of collards the night before, she felt it was nothing to stress about. That is, until she realized she was running a slight fever.

She remembered watching a news story about how some patients had experienced diarrhea before getting the full-blown virus, and she immediately went to her tablet to look the topic up once again.

As for the cats, it was Mona who brought her concerns about Brutus to the attention of Perilya.

"He hasn't moved all day," Mona told her, the unease obvious in her voice. " He feels hot and sounds funny, as if he can't breathe so good."

"It's funny you say that," Perilya told her. "Julia said she felt something in her chest. Something about it being hard for her to breathe."

"What should we do, Mom?" Mona asked.

"I don't know, but maybe we can get our Human to come take a look at him."

***

Still in her flannel nightgown and bathrobe, Earnestine rocked and watched the TV watching her as she pulled the blanket more tightly around herself. No matter what she did, she couldn't seem to get warm. Chills shook her body so much so she couldn't even sip the tea she'd made.

"Oh Lord Jesus," she shouted to the empty room. "Please don't let me go like this! Not by the Rona. Not by the Rona!"

Suddenly Perilya was at her feet, meowing and purring as if she wanted company.

"Shoo, cat!" Earnestine said. Even the short movement of her legs, trying to get the cat away from her, hurt. "I'm not in the mood to cuddle right now. Go!"

Both human and cat turned towards the doorway as Brutus staggered in, barely able to walk with his bloodshot eyes and running nose. He went directly to the human, never even acknowledging Perilya's presence in the room. He rose up, put his front paws onto her knees, and released a wet, forceful sneeze.

"These damned cats about to kill me." Earnestine whispered to herself. Despite the aching of her body and the burning sensation in her throat, she stood up quickly, knocking over her tea and went to the kitchen.

A year ago, Ja'Quan's wife had given her a few masks from the hospital where she worked, along with some rubber gloves. She had only worn the gloves once, right after the outbreak, on a trip to the grocery store, and since then they had stayed where she found them, up under the sink.

Back in the living room she picked Brutus up and immediately felt the heat of fever under his fur. Normally he didn't like to be picked up, but now his hot body only lay limp in her arms as Perilya watched him being carried through the kitchen and out the back door.

Why the Human had grabbed a funny stick from beside the refrigerator the matriarch didn't know, but one thing she was positive about: in the past she had only seen dead cats go out the back door.

***

"What was that noise, Ya?" Simon asked as Perilya came running down the hallway."

"I don't know!" She told him and the other cats who had come into the hall about Brutus being taken outside, just before the loud noise.

"Did the Human come back in?" Dillon, now the senior male in the house, asked.

"I don't know!" Perilya repeated. "After I heard the noise I came running up the stairs!"

"The Human killed Brutus," Julia said. She had come up behind them from Cat Room Number One. "I saw his face blow up."

"What do you mean?" several of the other cats asked as they looked at Julia's mangled fur, red eyes, and snotty face.

"You don't look so good, Julia." Simon said.

"And I don't feel so good. But I did see the Human blow up Brutus' face. I was resting in the window when it happened."

Suddenly they could hear slow, heavy footsteps coming up the stairs. It was their Human.

"Everyone hide!" Perilya ordered, and thirteen cats did as they were told.

***

Earnestine put the shotgun back beside the refrigerator and stood there debating her next move. She was eighty-three and all alone except for a dozen or so sick cats. She could call Ja'Quan and ask him to rush her to the hospital, but… but then she could possibly infect him or his wife and kids, and she couldn't have that on her conscience.

She reached for the phone on the wall, but stopped short of calling 911.

"What's the use!" She shouted towards the ceiling, "Earnestine Greeves, you done fucked up!"

She let out a series of dry coughs that felt like punches to her chest. Her body rocked so hard she dropped the phone and knew she would never be able to pick it back up. Earnestine was no bitch, and she knew what had to be done.

She forced herself to ignore how she felt and shuffled from room to room, grabbing one pistol from the living room, one from under the sink in the downstairs bathroom, and the last from under her mattress. All three hadn't been fired in decades, but she still remembered everything Ralph had taught her about guns back when they used to visit the shooting range just out of town.

In less than fifteen minutes it was done, feline fur and blood was scattered all over the house, and Earnestine had returned to the rocker downstairs to wait for the police to show up at her door. It took a lot longer than she expected…

LOVE IN A TIME OF EVERYTHING BEING A BIT SHIT

David R Mellor

There is nothing more unromantic than sitting on a park bench with, on a bench further down, "your date." The one and only one who replied, telephoning…

"Marg, it is Marg, isn't it?"

"Yes."

Stumbling for the first words, trying to get intimate…

"Urm..."

"Marg -"

"Yes."

"Do you have enough toilet rolls?"

To be honest I should have been grateful that anyone replied.

A few were interested but, on the day, cancelled, saying they had to "self-isolate," in one case for up to 6 months, following my persistent attempts to meet in 7 or 14 days' time.

The conversation was banal.

"Do you like socialising?"

"Yes. But I always keep a metre distance."

"I keep two."

This was the new six-pack.

"Yes, I got toilet rolls. But no beans! Couldn't find them anywhere, and shampoo sold out, would you believe it, who's so desperate for that? Bacon, milk, eggs, sugar, an endless drool of products each either in or out."

"Why don't you come a bit closer?"

She moved to the edge of her bench, still the recommended distance away. I looked at her. She was wearing jeans with a thick hooded coat, glasses, and a large surgical mask and plastic gloves.

In a bedroom I might have found this a bit kinky, but not here and now.

I noticed that she wasn't wearing socks and found this rather thrilling as though I was a Victorian gentleman.

"Should we go for a walk?" I inquired.

"Yes, that would be nice."

The prom was next to the park.

At first we walked behind each other, but we looked like mad men talking to ourselves. We decided to walk side by side but at a safe distance. The wind blowing fiercely.

"It's nice here." Lightening the mood.

"What!"

"I said it's nice here."

"Nice hair, ah, thank you."

"I think we should do it again." The last word fading in the air.

"What do you take me for? You men are all the same."

"No, I meant I want to come…."

"You are disgusting."

And in a matter of seconds the safe distance stretched to over a hundred metres as she walked into the distance.

I returned home deflated, useless, and pathetic. This was farcical.

Having been laid off at lightning speed by my social care employer, with a smile, as soon as the virus was mentioned, I knew I would have a lot of spare time now.

***

Deciding to take a break from the European championship of death tolls, I caught up with people.

"Hi Pete, hope you're keeping a safe distance from people?"

"Why?"

"The virus."

"Oh yeah, the flu can be bad."

(Another friend)

"No way I'm going to Mum's on Mother's Day, not safe. They're coming here instead."

(And Mum)

"Happy Birthday, you're not having a party tonight, are you?"

"No, God no... Just half a dozen or so friends coming over, but they will have separate chairs."

I put my head in my hands.

With the anticipation of a WW1 solider waiting to go over the top, I returned to the dating sites. Their numbers were also dwindling.

"Erotic" profile pictures of men, of women, half naked with toilet rolls and slogans like "love can beat the virus" and "let's self-isolate together, baby."

Then into my inbox came a message: "Are you man or mouse?"

Her name was Sass and in fact she appeared very sassy.

"Nothing can stop us."

"We can get close."

Within a few minutes we arranged a date at the same place as the others.

As I was leaving the house, I heard the news in the background...

"...only family members allowed out together; if you are a couple, isolate from each other, or move in together if serious..."

The words didn't sink in.

"We're alive, right?" She bounced along the prom like nothing had happened over the last few weeks.

"You see, we have a human need to be close to others."

I was sure she was closer than 2 metres, and at one point her fingers came close, almost touching my face, and I was sure I heard a cough. I secretly put hand sanitizer on my hands.

"You are sweet."

"Thank you," I replied.

"I mean, these new rules about only relatives from the same house being allowed out together, that's against civil liberties."

I nodded, having no idea what she was talking about.

"But that doesn't affect us," I explained.

"Duh. I'm black, you're white, if you haven't noticed."

At that point a police car was coming down the prom.

The police car stopped and two police officers started to walk towards us.

"Shhhiiiittt!" Sass looked panicked and scared.

"We've done nothing wrong."

Then a thought: oh God, she's a criminal, a drug dealer, a people smuggler, she's a prostitute; that's it, how stupid I was.

"Leave this to me," she said, regaining her calm.

"Nice day for a walk," the officer said sheepishly.

"Yes," Sass replied, beaming at my face.

"I suppose you've heard the news," the other officer said sternly, looking directly at me.

"Yes, all those deaths, terrible."

"No... I meant about only family members being allowed out together."

He appeared annoyed.

The cogs in my mind started to turn. There had been something on the news, but I couldn't pin it down.

"Yes, Officer, we did." As she threw a loving glance at me, I blushed.

"So, you are a couple?"

"Yes, Officer."

Wow, bingo, I thought; she's really fallen for me, and why wouldn't she?

"Actually, we've decided to move in together today."

If I had been drinking, the glass would have smashed on the floor

My brain screamed *nooo, well yes, but my house is a mess, the cat pissed on the sofa, and the piled-up dishes resembled the leaning tower of Pisa*.

"Have we?"

"Oh - you are being silly, dear..." (She'd forgotten my name). "We decided to move into your house in–"

"Wallasey," I jumped in.

With suspicions raised, the older officer enquired: "And why didn't you move into your partner's house in–"

"New Brighton," Sass cut in.

"Too big," "Too small," we said in unison

"Well...She thinks too small, I think it's too big." I had no idea what I was saying.

There was an awkward silence whilst the officers mulled over what we had been saying.

"Well, good luck to you both, and don't forget, only one walk a day." And off they went.

"Sass, I really like you, and if you want to live with me that's fine." Inside my heart was booming. A woman wanted me desperately, or she was desperate, it doesn't matter, either way I chuckled to myself."I just need to tidy the place up."

"What are you talking about? I've just met you, and that's a creepy thing to say; are you some kind of freak or something?"

"But you said – "

She was now over the required distance away, and moving further and further away.

"Didn't you see the news?"

"Urm, what, but you love me!" I shouted as she ran at a considerable pace into the distance.

For a whole day I sat in front of the TV soaking up the news till I was dripping with death, feeling seasick at all the graph curves going up, down, peaking, not peaking, my ashtray overflowing with anxiety, the empty cans of beer trembling in the corner with fear.

I broke the cycle by catching up with a few people.

"Yeah, we decided to move in together. In a way this is best thing to happen to me and Lucy - the government just pushed it along, I mean..." I cut the phone call short, as all this bathing in joy was sickening.

"Hey Pete, how you doing… Oh, you're going back to work soon, in the old people's care home. You'll need some protective clothing."

"What for?"

I smiled. Like a lamb, he was going to the slaughter oblivious of the reasons.

***

"Hi Mum, is all OK?"

"No… A resident brought a relative onto the camp. She was run off the site and tried to kill herself."

Now this was a welcome distraction.

My mother's idyllic caravan park had turned into a zombie apocalypse.

This whole "new" dating experience had left me wondering how anyone could meet anyone. Maybe, I thought, I should just hide in my hovel and re-emerge when this virus is gone. According to the latest saying, this could be on the 12th of Never.

But loneliness is a hunter, especially mixed with spirits late at night, and in my "not so dating" inbox, I saw a message.

"I want you... Let's meet, discreetly, we both want the same thing."

I had no idea what she or even I wanted but replied, "Yes yes yes."

Then I fell asleep in a drunken stupor.

I woke up early afternoon, a shiny P45 announcing that I was now unemployed waiting for me on the doorstep, and numbers after numbers on the screen.

Spain 900 deaths today, Italy 970 or something, America fucked, the UK staring at the virus like Bambi in headlights.

Her name, I found, was Fay, and she wanted me to come over to her house tonight as out and about was too risky. (Yep, I'd got that message now).

***

The house wasn't far, but as I approached it appeared to be in pitch darkness. With a trembling hand I knocked on the door.

"Come on in," a husky voice beckoned. A faint light guided me to what appeared to be a bedroom.

At one end, illuminated by a slight light, she sat, dressed in erotic underwear, her face dimmed. I sat rather foolishly at the other end, separated by the light of Darth Vader's saber.

"I'm not sure if it's two meters," she said, appearing to read my mind.

What the fuck am I doing here…

"We all need affection, don't we?"

I thought I recognised the voice but couldn't pin it down. Oh God, maybe she was an ex seeking revenge.

"Just relax… Do you want pleasure?"

"Yes... I mean, who doesn't?" I stuttered nervously.

"Pull your trousers down."

I obeyed like a naughty schoolboy.

"Oh, that's a nice package, mmm."

I went red.

Then two mop handles were placed like chop sticks around my....

"Ouch." One went into my stomach. "Sorry."

"Is that good?"

"It's different." This is not happening, run away.

"Now if you don't mind could you please me? Turn them round and run the mops over my breasts...Ohh yes, just like that."

It was a mop, to clean floors! How low could I go?

"STOP." I threw on the light switch.

The grotesque scene was illuminated by a 100-watt bulb.

"FRANK!" I tried to compose myself. "How's business?" Stumbling for words.

Frank Hearnes owned the hardware shop at the corner of my road.

"Bad, had to close due to the ban. Urm, sorry, I think the Darth Vader light saber is less than 2 metres."

"Not that, Frank, but this." The mop still on his chest.

"Well, I've always fancied you."

"I'm flattered Frank, but urm, I'll just go," I said, tiptoeing to the door.

"I've got those light bulbs you wanted."

"I'll pick them up sometime." I edged past the door. And in a flash, I was out of the house and home composing myself. That was it. I had to get a grip.

I turned on the local radio for some light relief.

"A Frank Hearnes has escaped quarantine at Arrow Park hospital. Do not approach him."

I sat back feeling hot all of a sudden.

In the morning I sat back and smiled to myself, seeing the funny side of everything that had happened. Then I was gripped with self-loathing nausea as I thought of just how self-centred I had become.

***

Marg, like all of us, was just frightened.

Sass was just fearful of all the changes that had happened.

Frank in his isolation had made a desperate lunge towards his desire.

And I was groping in the dark, literally in the last case. And my friends and family had their hearts in the right place; this virus thing had just spun them and their communities upside down.

I decided to give them a call…

"Pete, I 'm sorry, I just wanted to tell you the reasons why you need to protect yourself."

The conversation was long, but it finally sunk in.

"Thanks, Dave."

"It's all right. Stay safe."

And another…

"I'm really pleased your relationship is going well. You've had some awful times and deserve love."

"Thanks, Dave."

And Mum…

I turned to the leaning tower of plates, glancing at the overflow of weeping cans and ashtrays, and started washing. I knew I had to make one more phone call, to my wife. I started to uncontrollably sob, wiping my eyes with soapsuds, beans, and runny egg.

***

"Hello, it's me."

"Who is this?"

"Dave."

There was a stony silence on the other end. She was probably clenching her teeth.

"What do you want?"

A mixture of hurt and anger.

"I'm sorry…"

I waited for a reply. Nothing.

"I shouldn't have gone."

"I've heard nothing from you in three months."

"I know." Regret dripping off my tongue.

"You left me… (her last word hanging with a tear) to find yourself, saying you felt hemmed in."

"I know I was wrong; I just didn't realise how lucky I was with you, I was…" I didn't know what to say.

"You hurt me."

It cut through.

"Can we just meet up?"

There was a pregnant pause.

"Where?"

"The park bench – you know where. It's getting warm now and the flowers are coming up."

"Are they?"

The tone becoming lighter.

"And we could take a walk on the prom, but be careful - remember when the waves nearly drowned you."

"Yes, I remember."

And the conversation continued with laughter, love, and care, the ingredients which are central to life.

THROWING THE CURVE

R D Doan

Perseverance is such a fragile thing. It hinges on hope, nurtured by wisdom and patience. Too little hope, or too much without wisdom or patience, will only lead to despair.

Mark had taken care of several COVID-19 patients over the past few months. Most were put on ventilators, and less than half ever came off. His perceived failure as a medical provider weighed heavy on his heart. He had signed up for twelve weeks of temp work at Baymont Hospital working as a Physician Assistant in the ICU and step-down units. The work was grueling at times, but he had promised to stay until he wasn't needed. That was almost six months ago. The number of new COVID cases plateaued, but never slowed, so he never left.

Charlie had been admitted two weeks before with COVID-19. He was sent to Mark's floor for observation and quarantine and soon developed respiratory distress. As his health deteriorated, he was intubated and placed on a ventilator to help him breathe. Mark held little hope that this patient would be any different from the others. Something needed to change.

***

"Did you see that catch? He totally just saved that guy's no-no!" Charlie yelled to Mark from his hospital bed.

"Hold still, please. I'm almost done with this line. If you keep moving, I'll mess up and have to poke you again," Shelly, Charlie's nurse, chided. Mark could tell she wasn't too mad. There was a hint of playfulness in her voice… You really couldn't be that upset with someone who had just escaped death's grip.

"You don't understand. This guy's goin' for a no-hitter! Herrington just saved his ass!"

Shelly raised her eyebrows. "Language!"

"Sorry, ma'am." Charlie looked over to Mark and shrugged.

"All done here," Shelly said. "I'll be back in an hour to get vitals again and check the line. You just buzz me if you need anything, all right, sugar?"

Charlie nodded absently, his attention back on the game.

"Thanks, Shelly," Mark said as he entered the room from his post at the door.

Mark sat in a chair across the room, maintaining a safe distance.

"So, who's playing?"

"Padres and Dodgers in the NLDS! Man, don't you watch baseball?"

"Didn't even know baseball was back. But to be honest, I stopped watching when the Tigers traded Verlander away. When did baseball season start?"

"Back in June. Couldn't go to any games, though. They played in empty stadiums in Arizona at first. Teams were just starting to play in their own stadiums with restricted crowds just before I got sick."

"How can they allow teams to play in front of crowds with all the Stay at Home orders in place? Aren't they putting people at risk? Aren't they putting their own players at risk?"

"They're testing players and fans. I had a buddy who tried to catch a game at Comerica, and he said you couldn't get in unless you passed a screening at the gate. They were testing with those 15-minute portable testing machines or some shit."

On the television, a Dodgers batter took a third strike to end the eighth. Moore's no-hitter was still in play.

"Seems a little too soon for sports or large gatherings. If we push our luck, we'll end up with another surge of sick people," Mark said, shaking his head.

"Come on, man, the world needs baseball! We need a distraction from all this crazy shit. I mean, what else am I gonna do in recovery? It's therapeutic!" Charlie gestured to the television to illustrate his point.

As if on cue, a political ad for the President was running, touting the benefits of returning to "normal." It showed a clip from a rally where he bragged about how he had single-handedly brought back Major League Baseball. It showed an image of the President in a Yankees cap shaking hands with the Commissioner of Baseball at the White House.

"Yeah, sure. I guess having a distraction is good and all, but I still think it's too soon. We aren't over this virus yet. I'm worried about what'll happen when everyone thinks it's safe to abandon social distancing."

"Oh, relax, doc. It's not like they're playing in full stadiums. Only special people get to go to the games anyway. And from what I've seen on TV, they're pretty spread out, six feet apart and all that shit. They've even got masks with team logos on 'em!"

On the television, Ramon hit into a double play to end the top of the ninth. The crowd rose to its feet as the Padres took the field. Rookie sensation Jason Moore walked slowly to the mound to attempt something only done twice in history: to throw a no-hitter in a playoff game.

"I mean, come on, man; I'd kill to be at one of these Padres games. This is history in the making!" Charlie pointed to the TV again, as if Mark hadn't been paying attention. "They're playing with a team of unknowns and kickin' ass!"

"What do you mean?"

"Shit man, half the damn Padres were brought up just before the playoffs because half the team got the virus. Hell, Moore's only pitching in his third game!"

On the television, Hux took strike three as Moore recorded his first out of the inning. The crowd roared.

"Do you think they've got a shot to make it to the World Series?"

On the television, the announcer called the next at bat: "Well, that might be it, folks! A deep fly ball to center field. Herrington's going back… leaps at the wall… Oh what a catch! I can't believe it! What a play by the rookie, who does it again with a circus grab over the wall. Listen to that crowd. Moore must have an angel looking out for him today. With one out left, we're really seeing something special!"

Charlie shouted, "Yes!" and threw his arms in the air, pulling his new IV line out of his right hand. Medicine pump alarms went off. Mark jumped up, put on gloves, and held pressure on Charlie's bleeding hand.

"Did you see that catch?" Charlie asked. "That was some Sports Center Top 10 shit!"

"Yeah, just hold still a minute," Mark replied.

Shelly gowned up and came in shaking her head. "I thought I told you to be careful with that line. You can't be throwing your arms up with a line in your hand."

On the television, the Dodgers' last batter struck out swinging and the crowd went crazy. With one game left to win in the NLDS, the Padres looked hard to beat.

"So, Charlie, you said only special people can go to games. What constitutes special?" Mark asked.

"That's simple, man! You just gotta be rich!"

Shelly stood after applying the finishing touches on the new IV line. "That's not true. I overheard some docs this morning talking about a lottery. You could win tickets to see a World Series game."

"Yeah? How much you gotta pay to play?" Charlie asked, shaking his head.

"It's not like that. I heard they're giving away tickets to healthcare workers for one of the games. The docs were saying you just had to sign up through hospital HR. You should put your name in. You ain't got nothin' to lose."

"Hell yeah, doc! Put your name in and when you win, you can take me! I should be out by then, right?" Charlie beamed.

"Just rest up and do what you're told, and you just might get out in a week. We'll see," Mark replied with a grin. "We'll see."

***

Over the next few weeks, Mark continued to work long shifts treating a never-ending influx of COVID-19 patients, none of whom seemed to recover as fully as Charlie had.

He had exchanged phone numbers with Charlie upon his discharge and had called him several times to see how he was recovering at home. Each exchange between them started with pleasantries and a report on how Charlie was doing. He told Mark he was doing as well as could be expected. He was tired all the time, had a nagging cough and was still a little short of breath. His fevers were gone, and he said he felt better than he did while he was in the hospital. After the medical talk was out of the way, he always migrated to baseball. Charlie sounded more hopeful and alive when he talked about the game, and Mark was glad to hear it.

***

On a cool autumn morning, only a few days before the World Series was set to start, Mark was stopped by a security guard upon entering the hospital lobby. The burly guard ushered him into a nearby office.

"What the hell, man?" Mark asked the guard. "I was wearing a mask, so what's the problem?"

"There's no problem, sir."

"Then why the hell did you pull me in here?"

"Mark Wilson?" said a voice somewhere behind them.

"That's me." Mark turned to see a man in a suit standing behind them. "And who are you?"

"John Young, CEO and President of Baymont Health. And you, Mark, are about to become our hospital's biggest celebrity."

"I don't understand."

"A few weeks ago, you put your name into a lottery to win tickets to see a World Series game. Your name was drawn this morning. Congratulations. You're headed to Texas."

"Texas?" Mark asked, a little confused.

"The World Series is being held at a neutral site: Globe Life Field in Arlington Texas. So yeah, Texas."

Mr. Young sat down and motioned for Mark to sit as well. He continued, "I hope you understand, Mr. Wilson, that by accepting this prize you will be representing Baymont Health. From this moment forward, anything you say or do must align with the goals and ideals of this organization. If you are unable to comply with this, I am afraid your eligibility for this lottery may be in jeopardy. Do you understand?"

The only requirement for entering the lottery was to be a verified healthcare worker.

"If I promise to toe the line, I keep my job. Is that what you're saying?" Mark asked.

Mr. Young shrugged. "All I'm saying is that I want our hospital's representative to behave in a way that doesn't compromise our business. We stand to make a lot of money caring for COVID-19 patients so long as we don't upset the powers that be. The president's task force offers financial incentives to those who play well in the sandbox. As a representative of this hospital system, I don't want you engaging in any political discussions on social media or in interviews. Don't mess around in our sandbox."

"There won't be any issues, sir."

"Wonderful." Mr. Young stood up and smoothed the front of his suit. "As you know, your ticket comes with a companion ticket. Had you thought of who you'd take?"

"Yeah. A former COVID patient, Charlie Delmont. He's recovering at home now."

"Excellent choice. A healthcare provider taking a recovered patient to the game," Mr. Young replied. "Our PR team will love it. Now, let's go talk to some reporters."

The security guard opened the door for them both. Mr. Young stopped in the doorway, turned back to Mark, and said, "Smile, Mr. Wilson. You've just won tickets to the World Series. I'd think you'd be a little more excited."

***

When Mark called and asked Charlie to be his guest for Game Three of the World Series, Charlie was so excited that he went into a coughing fit.

"Holy shit, man! Game Three?"

"Yeah, sorry. I was hoping we'd see the opening game, but, you know, free tickets are free tickets, and..."

"No way, dude! Game Three is the best game!"

"Why?"

"Man, I swear. You don't pay attention to shit! Jason Moore is slated to start Game Three!"

"The kid from the Padres? The Padres are in the World Series?"

"Man, you been workin' too hard and need to get out more. Yeah, the fucking Padres are in the World Series! They playin' the Yankees, bro!"

Padres versus Yankees in the World Series. Mark thought that was just perfect. David versus Goliath. Good versus evil. That sounded just perfect indeed.

***

When Mark and Charlie touched down at Dallas/Fort Worth International Airport the night before Game Three of the Series, the news had already broken. Several players from both the Padres and Yankees had tested positive for COVID-19. According to reports, four Padres players and two from theYankees had tested positive for the virus but were showing no symptoms. It was also being reported that several family members from both teams were showing signs of the virus and were being quarantined just to be safe. Among the sick family members were Ron and Peggy Moore, the parents of Jason Moore, the Padres pitcher slated to start Game Three. Rumors questioning the validity of the tests soon spread as many fans voiced concern over potential roster tampering by both teams.

The next morning, roughly ten hours before Game Three's scheduled first pitch, Major League Baseball held a press conference at Globe Life Field to address the rumors and growing concern for the health and safety of players and fans. Seated at a long table were three men in suits, all sitting six feet apart. Aaron Johnson, the Yankees manager, sat on the left, while Joe Brinker, the Padres manager, sat on the right. Sitting in the middle, without a mask and wearing his standard blue suit, white shirt, red tie, and campaign smile, sat the President.

Beaming, the President addressed the nation. "Nobody loves baseball more than me. I'm the biggest fan, a tremendous fan. Everyone says so. It's true. That's why I brought it back. I brought it back. Me, I did it. And my Yankees are here in the World Series. We knew they would be here for this, a huge series, an important series. Of great importance. We needed to get back to normal. The economy around baseball is very important. I have friends, as you probably know, who employ thousands of people, hardworking people, that rely on baseball games to be played. We have the Padres. They're a bunch of little guys. The virus has been tough on them. No one could have predicted it hitting them so hard. But they're here. I'm sure it's an honor for them to be here. To play the Yankees. No one will look down on them for that, I will tell you.

"You may be wondering why I'm here talking to you today. Many networks, some good, most not so good, have said that the virus is back. It's all fake. We're beating this thing. Some people have said there were players who tested positive for the virus. I told my friend Hal Steinbrenner, you know Hal; I told him, maybe someone's trying to cheat. Maybe someone's trying to keep his players from playing." He shrugged. "I don't know. Could happen. I spoke with the Commissioner. We talked. I made a deal. That's what I do. As you know. I make deals. A tremendous leader makes deals. That's why you should vote for me in November. A Democrat couldn't have made this deal. Here's the deal. Tonight's game will be the last game of the Series. Winner takes all. We'll see which team is made of men and which team is made up of little boys."

The game would go down in history, and Mark and Charlie would be there to see it.

***

They arrived at Globe Life Field several hours early. Charlie wanted to soak in the experience as much as possible and watch some pregame batting and fielding. Mark was happy to see Charlie so vibrant and alive. He'd come such a long way from the weak and sickly young man who had come to Mark's floor so many weeks ago. He still coughed and got winded easily, but Mark could tell he was getting better. Baseball seemed to bring the best out of him, and for that, Mark was grateful.

They were leaning against the first-row railing along the third-base line while they watched the Padres take batting practice. They talked baseball for hours, until Charlie abruptly changed the subject.

"So, I gotta ask, man. Why me? I mean… why do all this? Why put your name in a drawing and split the winnings with a complete stranger? What did I do to deserve this? I ain't nobody, man."

Mark took a deep breath, sighed, and looked down to his feet. "Well, you helped me when I needed it most, so, I guess I'm repaying a debt."

"Help you? I ain't done shit, man! The way I see it, you helped me! You're the doc. I'm the patient. Seems pretty clear cut to me."

"PA."

"What?"

"PA. You said I'm the doc. I'm a Physician Assistant, a PA. Not a doc."

"Whatever, man. It's the same thing to me. I owe you my life, bro."

"Nah. I only played a part. There was a team of people who saved you. It wasn't just me. But you did save me." Mark put his arm around Charlie and said, "Let's get a bite to eat before it gets too crazy in here."

Charlie shrugged Mark's arm off his shoulder. "Not till you explain. What'd I do for you?"

Mark considered what to say. "Well, it's hard seeing people die. Especially in spite of all the work we do. Before you, I felt like I was failing everyone. There was just so much loss. You were my first recovery. Your gratitude, your joy, your acceptance, pulled me out of a dark place. I… Let's not talk about this now. Let's just enjoy the moment."

Charlie looked at Mark with a serious expression. "Sure." Then he smirked and said, "Let's go get us one of those boomsticks."

"You mean one of those two-foot-long chili dogs with jalapeños and onion? As your PA, I wouldn't suggest it," Mark replied, smiling.

"Well, you ain't no doc, so I guess I don't need to listen to you." Charlie smiled back as they headed up the stairs.

***

The President's ceremonial first pitch was thirty minutes late because he insisted on shaking hands with every player before he took the mound. For those watching the game from home, it appeared he was throwing a strike to a cheering crowd. In reality, he took two attempts to get the ball to the catcher under a cascade of boos. Fox, the only network allowed to broadcast baseball playoff games that season under the President's deal, dubbed in cheers over the boos and doctored the video. The commentators calling the game on TV praised the President for his athletic prowess.

The Yankees were considered the home team, so the Padres were first to bat. After a promising start with a double by Herrington, the next three batters struck out or lined out.

The Padres took the field to start the bottom of the first.

"Where's the pitcher?" Mark asked.

Charlie pointed to the bullpen. Jogging toward the infield came Jason Moore. The crowd clapped and cheered him out. There might have been more Yankee fans in the stands with most of the healthcare workers there hailing from New York, but everyone loved drama. The rookie pitcher was nothing short of sensational in the playoffs, and now he was pitching for all the marbles, with his parents in the hospital, no less.

Moore took the mound, squatted behind it, and wrote something in the dirt. He patted the message gingerly, kissed his fingers, and pointed to the heavens before taking the mound. He threw a few practice pitches to warm up, and the umpire called for the inning to start.

The Yankees' second baseman stepped up to the plate to start the bottom of the first. Moore looked to his catcher for a sign, nodded, and started his motion. The first pitch came in fast and looked like a sure strike, but the umpire called, "Ball!"

Moore shook his head in disbelief, collected himself, and stepped back on the rubber. The second pitch came in just above the belt, and the batter got all of it, sending it to deep center field. Herrington caught it on the warning track to record the first out.

"This is gonna be a long game for Moore," Charlie said. "That ump ain't doin' him any favors. The Yanks are gonna hit the hide off the ball if there ain't no strike zone. This is bullshit."

Next up were Gibney, who struck out swinging, then Torrent, who reached first after getting hit by a pitch. Moore's first two pitches to Stafford were on the outside corner, resulting in a foul ball on the first pitch, and a called ball on the second. This elicited boos from the crowd, who wanted a called strike.

"This just doesn't seem fair, does it?" Mark asked, shaking his head.

"It's bullshit," Charlie agreed.

The next pitch was a 98-mph fastball, right down the middle. Stafford swung and missed. Torrent took off for second and made it safely without a throw from the catcher.

Moore shook off three or four signs before he got what he wanted and stared down the batter with determination.

He threw another fastball, this time reaching 100 mph. Stafford nearly swung out of his shoes. The crowd cheered as Moore walked off the field. The tone of the game was set.

Over the next several innings, a pattern began to appear. Each team seemed to be playing with a different strike zone. The Padres had to deal with an unreasonably large strike zone and were left swinging at nearly everything. The Yankee batters were given a tight strike zone and were content to take balls all night long. Moore's craftiness on the mound, and the supportive plays by his teammates behind him, were the only reasons the game was still scoreless.

At the top of the eighth, Herrington hit a triple into the corner in right field. He showed off his speed as he beat the throw to third, sliding under the tag. Apparently, his effort had come at a cost. Herrington was replaced by Owen Gifford, a pinch runner, when he went into a coughing fit and had to be carted off the field.

On the next at bat, Titus laid down a squeeze play to perfection. Gifford dove headfirst ahead of the throw at home to score the first run of the game. The crowd went wild. Titus was on first with no outs and the Padres were up 1-0. After Greene struck out swinging, Castro came up to the plate. He swung on the first pitch and hit it to the second baseman, LeGrange, who fielded it neatly on one hop, tagged second, and threw to first for a double play. Just like that, the promising inning was over. But the Padres had taken the lead, and with the Yankees only getting one batter on base with a walk, Moore's no-hitter was still in play.

Moore stepped out of the dugout and made his way to the mound. Mark thought he looked a little peaked and was moving more slowly than earlier in the game. Moore threw a few warmup pitches and the catcher walked out to the mound but was shooed back.

"Something's wrong," Mark said.

"Yeah. He doesn't look so hot, does he?"

"I think he's sick."

"You think he's got COVID like his folks?" Charlie asked.

"Maybe. I don't know. He was tested before the game, right?"

The crowd was on their feet. Moore hadn't allowed a hit, and the crowd was starting to show their excitement. You could only stay quiet about a no-hitter for so long. Superstitions aside, if the kid could somehow survive six more outs, he'd be the first pitcher in history to pitch two no-hitters in the playoffs.

After getting Tannin to line out to left field to record the first out of the inning, Moore looked exhausted and his pitches were off. Urguay, the Yankees' third baseman, swung at the first pitch he was offered and hit a deep fly ball that landed in the upper deck in right field. It was just to the right of the foul pole. A long strike.

Brinker, the Padres manager, came trotting out to the mound to have a word with his pitcher. The conversation was brief.

"What do ya think that was all about?" Charlie asked.

"I think his manager is worried about him and wants to win," Mark replied. "Leaving him in there might not be the best idea. He looks like he could collapse."

"You think he'd really pull him? He's got a no-no goin'. He could be the first guy ever to throw one twice in the playoffs. Not to mention, I don't think anyone's ever clinched a World Series with a no-no either. Larson threw a perfect game in the '56 World Series, but it wasn't a clincher. I think it was the only other no-hitter in a World Series. If Brinker pulled Moore, he'd be stoned in the streets!"

"I don't know about that. I mean, look at the guy. He looks horrible. He must have said something pretty convincing to him."

With Urguay back up to the plate, Moore looked in for his sign, started his motion, and threw a curve ball that Urguay popped up foul along the third base line. Castro ran in and made the catch easily to retire the batter.

"Where the fuck did that come from?" asked Charlie. "I ain't never seen him throw a curve ball before!"

Moore was able to get the next batter to swing on three straight pitches, preserving his no-hitter. He looked tired as he slowly made his way back to the dugout. Mark noticed several other Padres players were moving slowly and coughing too. He recognized the symptoms all too well. They had all been exposed, and now they were starting to show symptoms. Mark wondered how many fans would start presenting with symptoms in a few weeks as a result of being there.

The Padres weren't able to get anything going at the top of the ninth, as Moore wasn't the only Padres player looking a bit under the weather. The first two batters looked outmatched as they feebly swung their bats.

"This is fucking crazy, man!" Charlie said between coughing fits.

"They're all sick," Mark muttered to himself in disbelief.

***

As the Padres took the field for the bottom of the ninth, several of the starters were noticeably absent. Second base, third base, and right field now all had replacement players. Mark watched Moore walk slowly to the mound and thought he looked so ill he probably shouldn't be out there pitching. He wasn't so sure the kid would make it through the inning without collapsing from exhaustion, let alone finish a no-hitter.

The Yankees were up to bat and Moore had the top of the order to contend with. LeGrange was up first. Moore's first two pitches were in the dirt.

"He's gonna have to throw a heater and hope for a fly out. There's no way he'll get him to strike out swinging," Charlie said.

Moore's next pitch was a fastball, only clocking in at 90 mph. LeGrange hit it hard to center field. Gifford tracked the ball back to the warning track and made the catch routinely to record the first out.

The crowd went nuts. Moore was two outs away from a no-hitter.

On the mound, Moore was bent over with his hands on his knees, looking beyond exhausted.

He took Gibney, the Yankees' next batter, to a 2-2 count and struck him out on another curveball. The crowd erupted in chants of "Moore, Moore, Moore, Moore!"

On the mound, Moore fell into a coughing fit before stepping back onto the rubber and striking him out on the next pitch. The crowd roared.

"One out to go! Can you believe this shit?" Charlie yelled to Mark.

Mark pointed to the pitcher.

On the mound, Moore dropped to his hands and knees. He was taking deep, heaving breaths. He shooed off the catcher and slowly rose to face his last batter.

"This is it. If he gets the out, he goes down in history. If he gives up a hit, he'll be yanked," Mark said. "I hope he's got enough gas left in the tank."

Moore's first two pitches to Torrent were fouled off, but his third pitch was hit hard. The ball was a deep fly ball down the third base line that hooked foul at the last moment.

Moore's last pitch was a breaking ball on the outside corner. To everyone's surprise, Torrent threw down a bunt.

The initial shock of it paralyzed both Moore and the catcher, but only for a moment. They both raced for the ball while the batter sprinted to first. Moore grabbed the ball and threw it for a bang-bang play at first. The stadium was quiet while everyone awaited the call. The first base ump seemed to consider it before he finally threw a fist in the air and yelled, "Out!"

The crowd erupted. In a mix of coughing and screaming, Charlie yelled, "Can you believe this shit! Best game ever!"

Padres players celebrated on the field, hugging and cheering, while Jason Moore lay unmoving on the first base line. EMTs rushed the field to aid the fallen pitcher. Other sick players were escorted off with oxygen masks. The scene was surreal, a mix of revelry and reverence. It was hard for Mark to watch.

Mark and Charlie watched the postgame press conference unfold from their hotel room.

Joe Brinker somberly sat alone to address the press. It was a stark contrast from World Series Celebrations of the past. He confirmed that Jason Moore, the 2020 World Series MVP, was being treated at Texas Health Arlington Memorial Hospital along with several of his teammates. Moore had collapsed as a result of respiratory distress, likely related to COVID-19. His prognosis was grave, with little hope he would survive.

"So, you still think it's time to return to normal?" Mark asked.

"All right, all right. Maybe shit like sports were brought back too soon, but you gotta admit that game was tight. We witnessed history tonight, bro!"

"Yeah, but at what cost, Charlie? At what cost?"

OR ELSE WHAT?

Eartha Watts-Hicks

The Woods family home at 146 Clinton Avenue already housed fifteen, putting it in violation of New York City's ten-person restriction. That would remain the case so long as Nan Christine, the matron of the family at age ninety-three, laid the law. Christine F. Woods was the signature on the deed to the two-family dwelling in the Bronx. Purchased in 1947, hers was a home that would always be open to family.

Tina returned like a prodigal daughter, after her whereabouts had been unknown for several months. She was permitted to shelter in place in the home that had belonged to the family for generations, despite her older sister's disapproval. "This is not a resort," Ellen said as she unlocked and opened the basement door.

Tina stepped in and saw her belongings against the far wall, boxed and taped up, and her furnishings dismantled as if waiting for U-Haul. Seeing that her mattress and box spring had been pushed into the dark enclave behind the washing machines was more of a shock. The unfinished basement ran the full length of the home with access to both the front and back yards. It served as their laundry room, where they hung the wash on their clotheslines. It was also a freeway for water bugs, silverfish, ants, spiders, mice, and squirrels. A wood broom stood against the wall, as usual. It did more than sweep debris into neat piles. It exterminated critters, but it never extinguished any of Tina's phobias.

Ellen, wearing a mask and gloves, planted herself some distance away from Tina. She said, "You have to isolate yourself from the rest of the household for three weeks."

"Or else what?"

"Those are the terms, Tina. You are welcome to stay if you remain in this house and in this basement for three weeks. And you are not to go upstairs for any reason."

"Ellen! Really? How am I supposed to eat? There is no bathroom down here! How am I supposed to bathe? How am I supposed to relieve myself?"

"Tina, let's not play games. When you're on the street, you cop your drugs and find a way to do all of that, even if you're out in plain sight. Here you have shelter, privacy, and running water. You can wash your ass in the utility sink. And you know that water is drinkable. And if you were so concerned about mice and bugs, you wouldn't have been living out there in those filthy streets during the pandemic to begin with. You smell bad. I don't know what you got or who you got it from."

"I'm not sick!"

"How would I know that? You could be COVID positive without symptoms. I don't know where you go, who or what you do to get your cash up for your next hit. I just know you showed up and stayed out in front of the house, screaming good and loud so Nan could hear you. And I'm supposed to roll out the red carpet for your bullshit?"

Ellen's angry gaze instantly made Tina regret returning home. "Don't look at me like that," Tina said. "I didn't choose to be an addict. I got addicted."

Ellen's deep sigh became its own statement. She looked directly into Tina's eyes before continuing, "In this house, I've got to take care of *everybody*! Nan, Uncle Joe, Uncle Bubba, and Auntie Rose. Adonis and Deana are the only ones helping me keep an eye on all the grands and great grands. Everybody else ain't trying to come in here. Lisa is an ER nurse. Pam is in Admitting. Julie is a CRNA. Rich is an x-ray tech. Mike is in patient transport. Chuckie is the head of maintenance at *his* hospital. They are all on the front lines. So they are staying where they are until this all blows over. You ain't got no essential work responsibility, but instead of being here and helping, you been gone. So, fine. When you left out of here, your bedroom became the Home Learning Center. We film and air some of our classroom lessons on YouTube. That is why we moved your stuff down here. Not because I was trying to shit on you. But it would be irresponsible for me to put you anywhere else but in this basement right now. And that's just being real. Either you accept it, or you don't."

Tina shrugged. "It's damp down here."

"It rains on the street. What do you want me to do, Tina? Risk the whole family trying to look out for you? Is that what you are saying to me?"

"No, but we used to lock the dogs down here like this! Ellen—"

"Three weeks!" Ellen grabbed a couple of comforters off the clothesline. Tossing them to Tina, she said, "Here! Make this work. There will be food for you at the top of the stairs in the morning and at dinnertime. If you're feelin' hungry in the middle of the day, send me a text. I'm taking care of everybody, all by myself. Now, all I'm saying might seem cold to you, but this is all I got energy for. I can't stop you from leaving again. But if you do, know this: I ain't letting you back in this house, no matter what Nan Christine says."

Tina nodded and watched as Ellen exited the basement. She heard the basement door shut. As Tina heard the door being bolted from the other side, a sharp pain seared her heart. Tina clutched the comforters to her chest, thinking, *This is cool for right now. I'll sleep here tonight. Tomorrow, I have to figure out my next move.*

***

Most of the family were essential workers. It made perfect sense to bring all the babies into Nan Christine's home where the elders and the babies could all receive care under one roof. The front bedroom became the Learning Center. Every morning the children tucked the trundle units back under the daybeds, shifted the futons back into place, and pulled out the snack tables to function as desks. Each child had an iPad and Wi-Fi access. Ellen purchased a whiteboard to make the room feel like a classroom. Adonis, age 18, and his 12-year-old cousin Deana tutored the younger ones and downloaded daily assignments to their tablets. As the younger children napped, the two older children began their lessons. Deana and Adonis studied well independently and received extra credit for the curriculum they watched on YouTube.

Adonis was a typical teen. He loved video games, basketball, and girls, hot girls. He'd entertain himself anywhere they were. Prophylactic-protected sex was his pre-pandemic pastime. By the time he returned home to wash the day's sweat away, he'd either be reveling in the memory of an earlier one-on-one match on the basketball court, or basking in the afterglow of a pretty female he had just met and drawn to him with his eyes and his infectious grin. Adonis was average height but had a magnificent build. His perfect posture toggled broad shoulders. Being snarky and abrasive was part of his charm. "Your hair is mad long. You ain't have to cut it?"

"Black girls get away with it. The shrinkage is real. Cops look at this shit and don't know what to think. Black female cops be looking at me like, *yeah, bitch I see you.*"

"Can I touch it?" Adonis asked.

"You could touch anything you want."

Adonis reached out and put his hands in her hair. He then brought his face mask to her ear and spoke softly. Sahara, the beautiful brown-skinned girl with freckles and kinky, naturally red hair, believed everything he said.

Adonis led Sahara into the basement and immediately caressed her. Sahara pulled away, noticing the enclave behind the two washing machines, "This bed is in a strange place, Adonis!" she said.

"So are you. So am I. So, why are you here?"

"I'm here because out of all the guys I've ever met named Adonis, you are the only one who actually *is* cute."

"I ain't mad at that," he said, stroking her shoulders.

On the disheveled piled of comforters, as Adonis peeled her clothing away, Sahara asked, "Do you have any condoms?"

"They're impossible to get right now. You know that. But don't worry. My pull-out game is strong."

"How strong?"

Adonis was staring into her eyes when he answered, "It ain't failed me yet."

In the strange enclave behind the washing machines, Adonis and Sahara pleasured each other, oblivious to ants, silverfish, or any spider crawling nearby. The young adults released their frustrations, cared nothing about the Coronavirus, and forgot about everything wrong in the world.

***

A week later, Ellen was in the kitchen, putting leftovers away. Adonis emerged from the bathroom, and his mother noticed the cough he couldn't shake. She stopped and rushed into the hall. "What the hell is that?" Ellen said to her son.

"Mom, you're overreacting! I'm good."

Ignoring him, she brought ginger tea with lemon and lozenges to his room. She placed the tray on his dresser.

"Drink this down. I'll pick up Vapor Rub and Castor Oil in the morning."

"Damn, Mom! Chill. All this you doing right now is extra!"

"Adonis, do you really think they would shut down the whole planet *this long* if this Coronavirus wasn't huge? White people may not like black people none, but they *loves* themselves some money! Our whole world done changed. School is YouTube, and there are no more church buildings. Women can't wear their hair long, can't wear dresses no more. There's a $1,000 penalty for going out without a mask and gloves. Fines for everything. And they got drones out there spying and emailing us tickets."

"Ellen!" The voice they heard traveling from the living room was Nan Christine's.

"I'll be right there, Nan!" Ellen yelled up the hall . She took a deep breath. "I'll be back to pick up that tray," she said, closing the door tightly.

Nine-year-old Shorty sprang from his pretend slumber. He leaned his head down from the top bunk. "Yo, Adonis. You been coughing. You think that pretty shorty gave you the Rona?"

"Mind your business, Shorty!"

"It's just a question."

"Yeah, and like I said, the answer is none of your business."

"You gonna drink that tea?"

"Nah, go ahead."

Shorty leaped down from the top bunk, just as Ellen swung the door open again. "And another thing," she said. "Shorty! Are you fucking nuts? If you bust your head open to the white meat, I'm going to be the one stitching your ass up! Ain't nothing but chaos in these hospitals right now! Your mother is doing all she can to save lives, and you in here flying around, trying to be an acrobat?"

"I'm sorry, Auntie Ellen."

"Now, I came back here to say I was a Girl Scout when I was little. My troop never went camping. There was never much appeal in a bunch of Bronx girls packing up to survive in the wilderness. We got our own dangers right here."

"Mom! Can you save this bedtime story for tomorrow?

"Listen to me! The point of camping, something I never understood, until recently, is to see how long we could survive without life's comforts. I work my ass off so that you could have it easier and have more advantages. What has that amounted to? Zilch. You're spoiled. You are eighteen years old and can't fend for yourself. This Corona Epidemic is the real deal. This is not a drill! And people who fail this test are dying. I should be able to send you to the store for bleach and detergent without worrying about you disappearing. I gotta make sure everybody eats, gets their meds, gets their bath; that these bathrooms and that kitchen stay clean; and that these kids stay *inside* and out of mischief."

"You see! That part! That's the part that I don't get. We got a front yard and a backyard. Why can't we just sit outside?"

"No yard! How long have you been jumping that fence, Adonis? How long have you been scaling that wall, running across the rooftops and up Tremont Avenue? If I say the backyard's okay, someone's gonna hop the back gate. If I say front yard's okay, someone's gonna be running back and forth to the corner store. These kids can stay right in here and pretend that banister is a roller coaster, long as I don't hear them. All right?"

"What you asking me for? You make the rules."

"Boy! Boy, if I had just a little more energy," Ellen pinched her fingers to demonstrate how much, "I would strangle you! But I gotta run out first thing in the morning to get everything we need to last through the next month. I'm taking the car, and I'm going over the bridge to see what I can find in Jersey. Make sure everyone stays in the house. Be sure to bring the packages in from the porch as soon as they get here. Don't let them get snatched up and stolen. This is what it is until the world opens back up. If I can't rely on you to do as you are told, we won't have *shit*."

*

Ellen returned home, exhausted. Deana, her, twelve-year-old niece, came barreling out when she saw Ellen pull into the parking spot in front of the house. Adonis hadn't come out to help. Ellen was annoyed but appreciated Deana. "We need to take these groceries inside. Wash the outsides of these containers before placing any of these items in the refrigerator or the cabinets."

"I know, Auntie Ellen," Deana said.

Ellen ran into the aroma of food as she neared the kitchen. The dishes had been washed, and the overflowing garbage can let Ellen know that everyone in the house had been fed, but Adonis had not dumped the trash. Ellen washed her hands and opened the cabinets to check the week's medication she'd prepared for the elders. Everyone had taken their morning and their evening meds.

Ellen closed the cabinet. She dropped her head and then turned to Deana, who was actively putting the groceries away. "Did Adonis help you at all?"

"No, ma'am."

"What did he do all day?"

"He was in his room all day."

Ellen opened the door to her son's room. Not seeing Adonis in his bed, she shook her nephew awake. "Shorty, where is your cousin?"

"He left," he whispered, still asleep.

"Did he tell you where he was going? Did you ask him?"

Shorty nodded his head. "He said, 'Mind your business.'"

Rather than upset herself, Ellen turned around and walked out. Everyone was fed and down for the night. She took a couple of Tylenol, showered, and went on to sleep.

***

The next morning, with waffles in front of him, Shorty had what Ellen called 'diarrhea of the mouth.' Between bites, he said, "He got a girlfriend. She real pretty. I heard them on the phone." Ellen wondered if maybe Adonis had run away from home. But then, Shorty said, "And he was coughing a lot. He told her his asthma was bothering him."

"Deana!"

Her niece rushed into the kitchen, "Yes, ma'am."

"Why are you covering for Adonis?" Ellen was miffed by Deana's childish shoulder shrug, and then the realization set in. "Adonis went to the emergency room. Did he ask anyone before he left?"

"No, ma'am. He said he was a man, and he could go by himself."

Ellen went for her cell phone and dialed Adonis. His phone rang until his voicemail recording played. *Hello, this is Adonis. I'm not able to answer this call right now. Please leave a message. Keep it brief or leave a text.*

"Boy! I hope you didn't go to that emergency room. And I hope by "emergency room "you mean Urgent Care. This is a damn pandemic. I do not want you in the emergency room or near the emergency room, and you knew that! If there is a problem, Urgent Care. But I do not even see why you would not call me or tell me to meet you at Urgent Care! I would have felt more comfortable if you told me where you were going, and I could have met you there. Either way, give me a call as soon as you receive this message." Ellen debated whether or not to say, "I love you." Not that she didn't love her son, but at that moment, she was aggravated. She ended the call with her thumb, stuck her phone in her pocket, and tossed her head back. The groan that left her body was a drone of aggravation, not pain. She was annoyed, but being annoyed, during this pandemic, was quite the norm.

***

Over the next couple of days, Ellen lost track of how many times she'd called Adonis. She assumed she'd killed his battery because the phone had started going straight to voicemail. Her son was missing, but the police refused to take a missing persons report because, at age eighteen, he was considered an adult. He would not be regarded as missing until two weeks had passed.

Ellen wondered if the police would be actively searching if Adonis was white and female.

She had been calling the hospitals, pressing 1 for English, getting placed on hold for hours. Just trying to get transferred to the emergency room, she wasted a day. Trying to get to patient information, she wasted two days. She was scheduled for overtime hours. No additional work was completed.

Deana knocked on Ellen's bedroom door and walked in with her iPad. "Auntie Ellen. His friends don't know where he is. But here is his Instagram page."

His last post was a dimly lit video, recorded in his bedroom. The lights had been off and the light shining on his face was emitting from his cell phone. *Hey. Yeah. I think I may need to go to have a doctor look at this and tell me why my toes look funny. This cough is hurting my chest. I know my body. But this doesn't feel like asthma, so I want to go check it out . . . just to be sure.*

Ellen looked over all the comments and friends that liked her son's last post. She typed in the comment thread from Deana's tablet. *HAS ANYONE SEEN ADONIS???*

It was a few minutes before @saharadessert replied. *No one has seen him for at least three days.*

It was then that Ellen realized she hadn't seen her son for three days. At the start of this pandemic, no one said or implied the kids would never go back to school. The Board of Education sent a per capita check for every school-age child. The sizable checks did not make up for the absence of an actual human teacher in the room to educate them. A virtual teacher or a hologram wasn't the same. Being primary caretaker of the elders, Ellen had gotten to a point where she wasn't checking on the kids five times a day anymore. She expected Adonis to knock on her door if something was wrong. He always wanted to update her while she was trying to get her own work done. "We were all adjusting to this madness," Ellen said to herself before she closed her eyes and tried to get some sleep.

***

"No one anticipated this pandemic would last this long. I mean, each and every one of us has to function around the clock and remember every detail when we're overwhelmed and exhausted. Who could predict the lasting effect this kind of trauma will have on our minds."

"Cuz. Cuz! Lisa! Adonis is missing."

"Missing?"

"Missing. I thought he might have run off with some girl. But it looks like he might have gone to one of the emergency rooms. He didn't call me, Lisa! Why would my son take his ass to a hospital in all this craziness and not call me? Why would he do that? Why? The fuck! Do I not say the same shit over and over to him fifty times?" Ellen sobbed quietly.

"Ellen. Ellen. Ellen, stop crying. Breathe. Calm down."

"I can't calm down. I don't know where my son is. And I can't really cry like I want to. I can't upset Nan,

Auntie Rose, and Uncle Joe. I gotta squeeze this pain down. But I'm gonna cry. Ain't no stopping that."

"This is crazy. I will call Chuckie. And Mike and Pam. We will get to the bottom of this, Ellen. Don't you worry. One of us will find out where he is. Understand me? We will find him. But for now, I need you to stay calm. Come on, let us bow our heads."

Ellen didn't know if Lisa's prayer would fix everything like magic. Still, the restful sleep she found afterward was nothing short of a miracle. The steady ringing of the bell jarred her, pulling her from her bed and down the steps. Wearing a thin nightgown that was barely modest, she swung the door open and saw a uniformed Police Officer standing there, wearing a face mask. "Ellen B. Woods?"

"Yes," she said.

"Sign here."

Seeing him produce a clipboard, Ellen didn't know whether to expect a search warrant or a warrant for someone's arrest. She signed by the 'X,' handed it to him, and stepped back so that he could enter the house.

The officer said, "No, ma'am."

He tore the pink duplicate from the form, bent, picked up a cardboard box and handed it to her with the copy. From his pocket, he retrieved a small object concealed in black plastic.

"I wish I had better news for you, ma'am. Take care and stay safe," he said, before tucking the clipboard under his arm, heading down the steps, and slipping into the driver's side of the tiniest squad car Ellen had ever seen.

Ellen set the box on the corner table while she locked the front door. She took a moment to remove the black plastic from the small package. It was her son's cellphone. When she realized the cardboard box was labeled Biohazard, Ellen felt dizzy and no longer had the strength to make it up the steep flight of stairs.

***

Ellen woke up in her bed without a clue as to how she got there. A mug filled with warm coffee sat on her night table next to her son's phone. She plugged her charger into the phone and sipped until the phone had just enough juice to be powered up. Once his cellphone came alive, she saw the 26 messages she'd left. But she also saw 33 messages from someone named Sahara. Ellen swiped to see the last SMS text message delivered to her son. It was also from Sahara.

Adonis! You need to STOP bragging on your pullout game! Your pullout game is weak AF. I am pregnant!!!

ASHES

Bill B. Peters

Six months after her death, John Ragland received his Aunt Thelma's ashes from the health department. They were incased in a nondescript urn, covered in bubble wrap, and sealed in what appeared to be plain brown meat-packing paper. The HAZMAT-covered delivery driver hadn't asked for a signature, but had simply left the package on the second porch step.

In the two years since the pandemic had begun nobody had been buried. Not even the rich could get around the Cremation Only Law. John's aunt had been his only relative, and he had inherited her wealth, including a $1.8-million-dollar home, dozens of upscale rental properties, and close to $11 million in cash. He'd loved his aunt about as much as any twenty-five-year-old construction worker could love a ninety-four-year-old jet-setting widow whom he saw, at most, twice a year. But since her passing had changed his life, he felt her remains deserved a coveted place in the house.

The fireplace mantel was cliché. No, the only proper place for the urn would be in the den, on the shelf above the old Victorian desk she had purchased from some far-flung corner of the world over a decade before anyone had ever heard of COVID-19.

John stood back, feeling somewhat proud of himself in his selection of location. Even with the quarantine being lowered to level 2, he didn't go out much, and with the den being his favorite room he'd almost guaranteed that he would see, and thus think of, his aunt every day.

"Rest easy, Aunt Thelma," he whispered to himself, just as her cat, Blue Blazes, jumped onto the desk and then onto the shelf, causing the urn to topple over and the ashes to scatter.

"Blue! You fucking idiot!" John shouted, but the indigo-eyed white ball of fluff didn't seem to notice as he rolled and tumbled in his former owner's remains as if they were a pile of catnip. "That's it, you gotta go! Tomorrow it's a trip to the tracks for you!"

John knew he didn't mean it. The cat was a pain in the ass, but it was Aunt Thelma's cat, and her will had mentioned Blue Blazes specifically.

John scooped up the mess as best he could with the small hand-vac, then dumped the contents back into the urn before returning it to the shelf. It seemed a little lighter this time, maybe because the cat's fur was no longer its usual bright white but was now a hobo-in-a-train-car gray.

***

"Wow, what a coincidence. My mom got Dad's ashes today too," Jenna said over the phone. "Maybe they send them out by zip code or something. Mom was starting to worry he'd been lost in the system somehow."

"Could be a zip code thing, I guess," John told her. "You want to come over?'

"You know we're back up to Level 3, don't you?"

"Since when?"

"Sometime last night. I saw it on the internet this morning. So no, I don't think I should visit. You in need?"

John sighed. Jenna Turner had been his aunt's housekeeper and all around Girl Friday, and after her death she and John had become close via their frequent phone conversations, eventually leading to a face-to-face about her coming to clean on a weekly basis. Over coffee in the kitchen, things somehow had turned into a pay-to-play arrangement. "In Need" was their G-rated code word for John being horny. "I'm always in need, but you knew that already. Are you sure I'm the only one you.."

"John! If you ask me that one more time, you won't be one at all! I told you, I'm not a whore for hire! It was a kinky fantasy of mine, and with the world changing because of this virus I thought it would be hot to live it out. It's just role-play for me!"

"Okay! Won't ask again! Geesh!"

"Plus, I'm a single woman living alone with my only regular human contacts being my mother and your dick!"

She hung up on him, and John considered calling her back to apologize but decided it would only make things worse. Better to let her calm down and reach out to him in her own time. Instead he called Grubhub and ordered dinner: steak and shrimp from Bilbow's Sports Bar. Until it arrived, he'd have a drink and smoke a cigar out on the patio.

The meow Blue Blazes emitted didn't sound right at all. John turned around to see the cat standing up on its hind legs and walking towards him in a jagged, drunken stagger. The gray ashes in Blue's coat were still there, but now they seemed to be moving, undulating, and flowing within the fur as if they were somehow alive.

John, always choosing to fight when flight was the other option, quickly came forward and kicked the cat halfway across the room. He continued kicking the ever-meowing feline through the house and didn't stop until he'd opened the front door and, with one last forty-nine-yard-field-goal-like effort with his left foot, sent the cat into the hedges across the lawn. Blue Blazes didn't move. John waited a solid twenty minutes to see if the cat was still alive, while attempting to control his breathing.

He called 911 and was then directed to Animal Control, who told him to put the cat in a bag and said they would pick it up within a few days.

"Fuck that!" he shouted back into the phone. "Did you hear what I just said? The cat walked into the room on two legs and looked like he was wearing a coat of dusty wigglers!"

"No need to shout, sir."

"I'm not shouting," John shouted into his phone. "Fine. Fine! A few days is fine! You have the address, right?"

"Yes, sir."

"Okay! Goodbye!" His body was tense with frustration as he hung up, grabbed a still-sealed bottle of Crown from the bar and a good cigar from the humidor, and then headed towards the patio.

The sun and warm breeze worked with the Crown to calm his nerves. By the time his order had arrived a good amount of the bottle was gone and he felt pretty mellow. He ate the entire meal on autopilot. One minute he was unpacking the deliciously fragrant contents from the black plastic bag, and a moment later he was belching over a paper tray with nothing left but the cleaned bone of a medium-rare rib eye and several shells which had previously contained jumbo shrimp. There was no trace of the huge baked potato.

***

"I was just about to call you, John!" Jenna semi-whispered into the phone. "I'm at Mom's, and she's… Acting. Funny."

"Funny how?" John asked. "Has the quarantine finally got to the old diva?"

"I'm serious. She's right behind me so I can't talk, but can you please come over?"

John got out of bed and jumped into the shower. Two days earlier he could have left home simply wearing an N95 or equivalent face mask, but with the Official Quarantine Level being at 3 now, anyone leaving their home was required to be in full HAZMAT, including face shield with attached hood, heavy polymer blended plastic gloves, jacket, and over-pants, as well as galosh-style, knee-high over-boots. Initially this outfit seemed to be the cause of increased traffic accidents and eventually led to a minimum distance of four vehicle lengths being required when traveling in the city, except for people in the act of parking. Not only was the world getting used to staying in, but those who went out were also getting used to driving at a maximum of twenty-five miles per hour.

When he arrived at Bethany Anne Turner's apartment, Jenna met him at the door. The look in her eyes behind the mask she wore showed even more concern than had come across in her earlier phone call. It was obvious she'd been crying.

"I don't know what happened!" Jenna sobbed, a fresh round of tears soaking her mask. In a normal world, John would have held her in his arms and tried to assure her everything would be all right, but even though they were sexual partners, both were used to the new social/personal space protocols and standards the coronavirus had forced on everyone.

"What exactly is she doing," he asked?

"She's in there crushing up charcoal briquettes now!"

"Charcoal briquettes? Like charcoal for a barbeque?"

"Yes! And before that she was breaking up every pencil she could find in the apartment!" Jenna fell into John, not seeming to care about social protocols anymore. She began to cry uncontrollably, and he wanted to take off his HAZMAT suit and hold her, skin to skin, like he did when they were intimate. Nothing in the moment seemed right with the suit on. He let her get it all out before telling her to stay on the porch while he went inside.

The apartment was one of those excessively efficient spaces reserved for college students and senior citizens with living assistance needs: small kitchen to the right, living room to the left, with a bedroom, bath, and sometimes laundry down a narrow hallway.

John went into the living room and found Mrs. Turner on the floor wearing a tattered flannel housecoat. Her back was against the front of the sofa and her legs spread underneath the coffee table. Beside her were two twenty-pound bags of Kingsford charcoal, one tipped on its side, empty, and the other appearing to still be full. Mrs. Turner shoved her right hand into the latter and attempted to bring out a fist full of briquettes, but her tiny hands could only hold two at a time. She raised the charcoal above the table and ground the pieces together with a strength John found hard to believe. The briquette's crumbs were added to the already huge pile in the middle of the coffee table, and at their center was an urn.

"Oh shit!" John said inside his HAZMAT hood.

For the first time, Mrs. Turner seemed to acknowledge his presence in her home. She turned her head and stared as if it wasn't her on the surface, but deep within her wary eyes, John could tell she was in there, tired and afraid. Her mouth slowly began to quiver, and finally was able to speak the words, "Help me!" Her voice, which sounded as though she had a sore throat well on its way to becoming a chest cold, was raspy and barely audible through the layers of HAZMAT suit.

"What's wrong with my mom?" Jenna said from the back side of the couch. She sounded like a little girl. "Is she going crazy?"

"I think your moms' sick," John said flatly. "Do you know if she touched your dad's ashes?"

"Yes, I know because she told me when they arrived. She said she missed him so much she just wanted to touch him. I thought it was romantic. Why?"

He told her about Blue Blazes.

***

Within twenty-four hours the Official Quarantine Level for the United States had been raised to Level 5; no unauthorized movement outside the home for anyone, including all emergency personnel and first responders. Americans were ordered to shelter in place. Unmanned security forces including, but not limited to,

AI robots and drones would have the authority to kill on sight until the level dropped back to 4 or below.

The leading Internet conspiracy theory, based on audio and video testimony, was that, at least for the United States, the "virus" had been more than just a virus - had actually been part of the cover-up of a carbon-based nanotechnology trial gone wrong.

As the coronavirus began to spread across America, programmed nanobots had been released to enter the bodies of a random sampling of the populace and to disrupt the human respiratory system until death occurred. Unlike real pandemic victims, these individuals were to be sent to a special laboratory run by one of the world's largest and most powerful military contractors. There the bots would be magnetically removed and the bodies studied. If all went well, America and her allies would have a new powerful weapon at their disposal.

Unfortunately, many of the bodies were lost or cremated locally before federal authorities could take possession of the remains. This led to hundreds of cremations, which the Nanobots naturally viewed as an attack, an attack against which they were intelligent enough to defend themselves against.

NO WAY TO KNOW
Anna Lindwasser

"This is stupid," grumbles Jesse Berkowitz's 12-year-old daughter Noemie as she toes off her turquoise Mary Janes and kicks them across the hardwood floor. "I was supposed to go trick-or-treating with Allison and Lillie, but I guess what I want doesn't matter, huh?" She crosses her arms. "Why do we have to move to the middle of nowhere?"

Jesse's wife Miette gives the child a look that could make an onion cry, prompting her to put her shoes on the shoe rack where they belong.

"Ask your father," she says, pushing the stroller into the living room and unzipping Simon from his duck-patterned sleep sack.

"I wish you wouldn't act like I'm being unreasonable when I'm just taking the same precautions that everyone should be taking."

"Let's not fight," Miette says as she stretches her long body out on the blue plaid couch. She picks up Simon and coaxes his toothless mouth towards her nipple.

Jesse sighs. "Fine. Noemie, could you help me bring in some things from the car?"

Noemie follows him out to the car, monologuing the whole way about why living upstate will be a disaster: she'd been planning to audition for her school's winter concert, she's horribly allergic to the mold that collects in the dead leaves of trees, he's delusional if he thinks he'll find another job in the middle of a recession. He doesn't love the complaining, but he gets it. He hadn't wanted to leave home during the COVID-19 outbreak, either, though he'd been too young to know what a recession was.

When Jesse was six years old, he held his family's border collie by the collar so she wouldn't run over and bark at the hole their dad was digging in the yard. The hole would later turn into a well that would end their reliance on the public water system.

This wasn't the only thing that the Berkowitz family did to keep themselves afloat during the pandemic. They created a vegetable garden and started raising chickens. They put solar panels on the house, got a solar generator, and bought a massive freezer to keep all the food they'd need to wait out the quarantine.

At the time, Jesse thought that all those preparations were overkill. He couldn't imagine his family using up one 50-lb bag of rice, let alone ten of them. He didn't get why they suddenly had more toilet paper than they could fit in the closet or why they had to wash their hands after every time they went outside. He didn't want to leave Brooklyn Heights and move permanently into their vacation home, or clean out the hen house when he could have been playing Minecraft with his friends.

But when the grocery stores closed and water no longer flowed from the tap, he didn't complain anymore. When the whole family started coughing and they had to bury his father in the backyard because 911 no longer led anywhere, he knew they'd done the right thing.

Later, when it was all over, he made his way back to Brooklyn. Some neighborhoods roared back to life, while others stayed boarded up and desolate for years. It took some time for Jesse to find a job, but he eventually became a barista, then a manager. That's where he met Miette - she came in a couple times a week to drink rose matcha lattes and draw what he later learned was a comic strip about vampires.

Eight years younger than Jesse, Miette was born after the wounds from COVID-19 had been more or less healed. Now, with news of another pandemic on the horizon, she isn't worried - at least, she isn't worried down to the marrow.

That's why when he decided to move the family to the upstate home he inherited from his parents, she fought him on it.

"We can't take Noemie out of school," she said, arms crossed as she leaned against the refrigerator. "She's been studying her butt off to get into Brooklyn Tech. We can't take that away from her."

"By the time the pandemic hits, there might not be a Brooklyn Tech," said Jesse. "Look, I know you don't get it. It's okay that you don't. In fact, I don't want you to. You can't understand unless you've been through it. That's exactly what I'm trying to prevent."

"It's not that I don't understand, it's that I hate it," she said, nails digging crescents into the flesh of her arms. "You waste your life preparing for a disaster that may never come, and now you want to waste your family's lives, too."

"You'll thank me when society shuts down but you're in a warm house with food on the table." Jesse shoved his hands into the pockets of his khakis.

"You can't prepare for everything. You think that you know how this will turn out, but you don't."

Jesse didn't say: if we don't learn from history, we die, but he thought it so hard that it took up all the space inside his skull. They didn't talk about it anymore, and Jesse started making plans for them to leave. Miette protested every once in a while but took an online gig writing business copy that could travel with her upstate. She hadn't liked it, but with Noemie's health issues and Simon's age, she was probably scared too.

When Miette finally brought it up again, they were lying in bed together, Jesse combing his fingers through his wife's curly brown hair.

She said, "I think we should bring a gun."

"Are you insane?" He stopped combing and grimaced. "Why would we bring a gun? Neither of us have ever held a gun in our lives."

"You haven't held a gun. Don't make assumptions about me."

Jesse was about to protest that she'd never told him about any history with guns, but Miette was onto another subject.

"There are wild animals up there," she said. "What are we going to do if a coyote gets a hold of Simon?"

"That won't happen - bears are friendly."

"They are not!" She flicked him just below the nipple; he batted her hand away. "If they were, there wouldn't be a whole Wikipedia page dedicated to bear attacks."

"The fact that a few people in history have been killed by bear attacks does not mean we should have a gun in the house with two kids."

Miette rolled over and pressed her face into the pillow. In a muffled voice she said, "I'm scared."

"Of what - bears?"

"Yes, bears! But there are other problems too. How am I going to get my work done while I'm taking care of a baby and a recalcitrant pre-teen? What if I can't figure out how to start a garden, or the chickens peck Simon's eyes out?" She drew her knees to her chest and took a raggedy breath.

Jesse tried to tell her it would be okay, but she kept talking. "Is the local grocery store going to have Ample Hills ice cream or am I going to have to eat Turkey Hill? What if all of our neighbors vote Republican? How am I supposed to get my tattoo touched up when it fades? Living in the woods is going to be terrible for Noemie's allergies – did you even think about that?"

He tried to interject that they had plenty of medication for her, but before he could the subject changed again.

Miette finished off her rant with, "We still don't even know what happened to Ruth Ann. What if a serial killer got her and he's still lurking around in the woods? What are we going to do then, Jesse? How is a lifetime supply of rice going to help us then?"

"The first thing we need to do is stop dreaming up worst-case scenarios," Jesse said, his voice tight. Bile rose in his throat, and he wanted to scream. How dare she use his mother's suicide as a bargaining chip? But he said nothing. He tried to comfort her with a gentle pat on the shoulder.

She flinched. In a cold and quiet voice she said, "I'll stop when you stop."

Despite the arguments, they're moving. Now they're arriving at the summer house, and they have a lot of unpacking to do. Aside from their personal belongings, they also have supplies. They have N95 respirators, Lysol spray and wipes, hand sanitizer, antibacterial soap, and toilet paper. They have two 50-lb bags of rice and as many cans of black beans and bags of frozen mixed vegetables as they can fit in the cooler. Diapers and gardening supplies and acetaminophen. As many refills on Noemie's medications as he could get: Imuran, Symbicort, Claritin. A drum of gluten-free brownie mix, for their sanity. Cash in case the banks go down. Plans to head to the local Agway and get supplies to get the garden going in the spring, and the phone number of a local woman who promised to sell them chickens to replace the ones that ran away after his mother disappeared. No weapons, because having weapons in the house with two kids is unsafe.

It's not enough, but that's okay - they're not on lockdown yet. The potentially pandemic flu strain that's been in the news is still primarily affecting Europe. It'll get to New York, but they have time to get settled before that happens.

Unloading the car takes about two hours, and when they're finished, they have to make dinner. Jesse drove up a few weeks ago to make sure the power was on and the well was functioning, and to clean up all the dust that was clinging to the crockery which he now uses to make gluten-free linguini with chicken sausage and broccoli while Miette helps Noemie with a math packet that she found on a homeschooling website. They listen to Pinback, a band that Jesse's mother used to listen to before she died.

Being here without his mother is harder than Jesse expected. He processed his father's death a long time ago, but his mother's was recent and shocking.

About six months ago, she abruptly stopped replying to his messages. He drove upstate to check on her. When he arrived, the front door was swinging on its hinges. There was a bag full of rotting produce on the counter, and the chickens were gone. A police investigation had turned up nothing, and the case was dropped.

Jesse was pretty sure it was a suicide. She hadn't bounced back from the outbreak the way that Jesse had. Per her description, losing her husband was like having all of her limbs chopped off and then having to act like she still had them. She never tried to date again or took off her sapphire wedding ring.

She never moved back to the city even when it was safe, and she maintained none of her friendships. Jesse tried to visit, but she nearly always turned him down.

She talked about not wanting to get out of bed, about washing her hands so often they bled. She talked about spiders that she saw but knew weren't there.

He'd hoped that when he moved up here to outrun the pandemic flu they could reconnect. Maybe he could persuade her to start using the remote therapy subscription he'd bought her. Maybe she'd finally be able to meet her grandson.

Part of him still hopes that she isn't dead, just missing. But that isn't his focus. His focus is keeping Miette and the kids safe.

They will be safe here - safe and happy. Compared to the city, the Catskills are beautiful: nobody drilling into the sidewalk outside their window, no light pollution blocking out the stars. Jesse looks up from cutting the chicken sausages into fourths to look out the window.

The sky looks like graphite, and there are no stars. That's okay - the forecast for tomorrow is clear. Tomorrow, he can show his family the small pleasures of their necessary move.

"Dinner's ready!" he calls, signaling Noemie to start setting the table and Miette to try and strap Simon into his baby seat without getting protest-kicked. It takes some time, but eventually, they're all seated and digging into their meals.

"I hate gluten-free pasta," says Noemie, twirling the noodles on her fork and glaring at them. "Why can't we just eat the regular stuff?"

"Because, sweetheart, you have celiac disease," says Jesse. The words feel heavy in his throat, but he reassures himself with the fact that as long as they're here, he has full control of her diet. He's more concerned about her asthma, and what will happen to her lungs if the pandemic flu finds them here.

Noemie rolls her eyes and kicks out her feet but stuffs a bit of pasta into her mouth. She starts talking about a virtual reality gaming system that she wants to buy. "If we're going to be stuck here for months you should at least let me pretend I'm somewhere else," she says.

Before Jesse can respond, Simon sends his plastic baby bowl of pasta sailing onto the floor. Jesse gets up to retrieve it, but as he's getting up from the floor he notices a strange, hulking shadow in the window. He blinks, and it's gone.

It's probably nothing - maybe he's just tired from the trip. He shakes his head, dumps out the ruined pasta, and ladles some more into another plastic bowl. Hands over the food, tries to focus on feeding his son and making silly faces to coax a smile out of him. He wants to see that toothless grin, because his wife and his daughter are both frowning hard and there's nothing he can do about it.

It's okay, though, because protecting his family is more important than anything else. That's true whether they understand it or not.

He stoops down to clean the pasta from the floor, and then he hears Noemie scream.

Electricity shudders down his spine, and he scrambles to her side. "What's wrong?" he says.

Noemie points out the window closest to the table, one hand clapped over her mouth. Her brown eyes are wide and wet with tears.

She gasps, prompting Miette to push her inhaler into her mouth. After a puff that leaves her breathing ragged but controlled, she yelps, "Giant spider monster!"

"What are you talking about?" Miette says, hands gripping Noemie's shoulders. "There's no monsters. Maybe you've been playing too many virtual reality games already if you think that."

"No, Miette, I saw something too," says Jesse. The word *spider* makes him feel like he's swallowing gravel. "Over by the other window. I'm sure it's not a monster – maybe she saw one of our new neighbors?"

"If our new neighbors have millions of glowing eyes then I am running back to Brooklyn." Noemie grabs Jesse's arm, her fingers leaving red marks in his flesh.

"I'll go out and see what's going on," he says, shaking his arm from his daughter's grip.

Miette walks over to the sink and retrieves the chef's knife he'd been using to chop the sausage. "Take this," she says, pressing it into his hands.

"I don't need a knife, Miette."

"There are bears and coyotes out there. Just take it." Her eyes are flinty, open wide.

"Even if there is a bear or a coyote, it won't do me any good. I have no idea how to fight with a knife. I'll probably just drop it and stab myself by accident."

He knows that taking the knife will bring Miette peace of mind, but he's less worried about her piece of mind and more worried about looking like a maniac in front of what are almost certainly the neighbors.

He slinks out the door with no weaponry in hand. Closes the door behind him. With no stars to light the way, he turns on his phone's flashlight, aiming it first at the house, then at the car, then at a gnarled tree, then at the car-sized million-eyed spider clinging to the tree.

Before he can process what he's looking at, the spider launches itself at him like a firework, knocking him to the ground and dragging him along a path of roots and leaves and rocks. A bloody hole opens up in his cheek. He can hear his daughter screaming in the distance, but it's a quiet sound over the shrieking hiss of the monster. He tries to grab its leg and loose himself, and when that doesn't work he tries to scoop up some gravel and hurl it in the monster's direction. It roars so loudly he can hear it over the sound of his pounding heart.

Before he can process it his body is a Frisbee slicing through the air. He tries to scream but his lungs squeeze shut. The spider pins him to the ground, blocking his vision with the thousands of glowing yellow eyes bubbling out of its head.

He tries to kick it in the thorax but, just before his foot connects, his leg goes limp.

The spider's fangs are buried in his shoulder. The pain crackles through his entire body, making his muscles cramp, and his blood feels slushy and cold. Drool slithers from the corners of his mouth, and his hands shake so hard it feels like they're about to launch off from his wrists.

He manages to turn his head to the side. His vision blurs, but when it clears he sees a dark shape on the dirt ground. It smells like rotting cabbage mixed with shit, and its shape is alarmingly human. He retches. It's a woman, one who seems to have been dead for some time. Her ribcage is cracked and her chest cavity is filled with clusters of orange orbs. Each one is the size of a fist. They're too smooth to be viscera - could they be eggs?

His first instinct is to squeeze his eyes shut. He's going to end up just like this person in another minute or two. It's not going to do him any good to see that future - it'll only distract him from the possibility of escape.

But if he doesn't see what happened to that person, he won't know what's coming next. He forces himself to open his eyes. When he does, they land on a streak of sapphire blue. A jewel on a rose-gold band.

That detail puts the rest of the body into focus. That's his mother's wedding ring. The one she used to stare at while tearing up. The one you'd have to sever her hand to take off.

His mother. That's his mother. Most of the flesh on her skull is missing, but that's her. Beneath the cavern in the woman's chest is a bloodstained purple Merino wool cardigan. Jesse knows that it's Merino wool because it's the cardigan he bought for his mother at the Rhinebeck Sheep & Wool Festival five years ago. She'd loved it, worn it every day. Now it's stained. Her ring is stained. Her face is gone. She's dead.

Jesse tries to kick again but finds that his legs are bound. Spiderwebs. Those are supposed to have the tensile strength of steel. He can't move his legs at all. Can't move the rest of his body without every part of him screaming in pain. He's going to die here. Die alongside his mother. This monster is going to kill him and then go after Miette and Noemie and Simon, and everything he's ever loved will be gone.

Then, just above the spider's shrieking hiss and the sound of his own bones cracking, he hears the screech of wheels and the roar of an engine. He turns his head, ignoring the sting of pain as the spider's fangs saw through his skin.

The window opens. The barrel of a gun peeks through. A shot shatters every sound in the world. The bullet lodges in the spider's cluster of eyes. Fluid sprays everywhere, and the spider reels back, its teeth dragging down Jesse's neck before it disentangles from him entirely. Another shot and its legs flail wildly. Another shot and it stops moving.

The car door opens. Miette tumbles out of the driver's seat, wild-haired and demon-eyed. Pistol still clutched in her right hand, she whips her way towards Jesse and grabs him under the armpits. She's saying something, but he can't hear her. Then he's slumped in the passenger seat, his head pressed against the window and his heart drumming in his chest.

He can barely hear anything over its relentless sound, but he feels the car begin to move. He can feel the pressure of his daughter's knees on the back of his seat. His eyes are shut, but the light changes as they move from the woods onto the highway. They're moving.

***

Jesse wakes up covered in bandages and leashed to an IV pole, bright hospital lights beating down on his eyes. He groans and tries to sit up, then falls backwards onto his pillow.

He turns his head and sees Miette sitting by his bedside, Simon asleep on her lap, his drool decorating her sea-green blouse. Noemie is sprawled across a plastic chair, frowning at her cell phone. She puts it down and scuttles over to Jesse. Throws her arms around him and yelps, "You're alive!!"

Miette pulls her back, not with movement but with a flinty glare. "Noemie, be careful not to hurt your father."

"Sorry." Noemi steps back, then bounces on the balls of her feet. "I was just so worried about you!"

It takes some experimental croaking and swallowing, but he manages to force words from his throat. "Did you see what happened?"

"Yeah, we were in the car with Mom. A giant spider almost ripped you in half! But then Mom shot it until its head exploded and saved your life!"

"That's pretty cool…" slurs Jesse, staring at his wife. He'd been so sure that he'd be the one to save her from the virus. He'd never expected her to save him from anything.

Miette blushes and bites her bottom lip. "Like I said, I know my way around a gun - I used to do target practice in high school. Before we left the city, I bought a Beretta PX4 Storm."

Jesse doesn't know what that is, other than the fact that it's a pistol. "Because of the bears?"

"Because of anything that might threaten us. I figured you had all the household problems covered, so I'd take care of this." She sighs. "You weren't receptive to the idea, so I didn't tell you."

"Mom, tell him about where the spiders came from!" Noemie says, arms windmilling in front of her. She's clearly excited, though in his painkiller haze he can't imagine why.

"It's pretty unbelievable," says Miette, adjusting Simon who is starting to slide off her lap. "Apparently, their DNA was mutated by a virus: their offspring were enormous and they laid their eggs less like typical spiders and more like botflies. Most of them had been using animal corpses as nests, but a few started using human bodies. That's what they did to Ruth Ann. It's what they were trying to do to you."

His stomach flips like he's about to vomit, but nothing comes up. His brain is a slurry of horrible thoughts, and it's nearly impossible to fix on a single one long enough to respond to it.

"This is why I said that you were focusing too much on the pandemic flu," says Miette, threading the fingers of her free hand through his. Her voice is calm, but he can feel her hands shaking.

"A virus did cause it, he's not totally wrong," says Noemie, doing the same thing to her brother's tiny hand. "And people are still getting the flu - that hasn't stopped happening just because there are spiders now."

Jesse appreciates his daughter's support, but Miette is right, too. He had not predicted everything. He couldn't have. Nothing in his reality had pointed to the existence of mutant spiders at all. In a world swirling with terrifying unknowns, he cannot possibly protect his family from harm.

"We can't stay here," says Miette. "The woods are full of spiders, and exterminating them could take months. So, we're going to drive out to Ohio and stay with my sister. I'll have everything arranged by the time you get out of the hospital."

"How do we know that it's safe there?" he asks, his voice cracking at the end of the sentence.

"There's no way to know that, Jesse." Miette shuts her eyes and breathes out through her nose. "We just have to be strong enough to handle whatever comes next."

Eyes closed, he murmurs his agreement.

CROWDFUNDING THE APOCALYPSE
Katia Kozar

Everybody has a sob story. "I lost my job during the pandemic."

"I got evicted during the lockdown."

"I couldn't get my medicine during the stay-at-home period."

Boo fucking hoo. Why should anyone care what your problems are? They've got enough problems of their own.

And that's a problem for me. Because I need a job.

Before the virus hit, I made a living as an editor cutting porn for an independent outfit located in the San Fernando Valley. The money at Online Orgasm sucked, but it was enough to pay my rent and keep me supplied with necessities—weed, food, and my monthly subscription to *World of Warcraft*.

And they even paid for my lousy health insurance, which was better than nothing because I've got high blood pressure and need to take statins, which you can't exactly get over the counter. My girlfriend Rena swore eating beets and oatmeal would take care of the problem, but Rena said a lot of dumb stuff. Before the plague she was a yoga instructor who consumed a lot of sketchy information from self-proclaimed "nutritionists." She had a supply of bottled supplements that took up one whole shelf in our tiny bathroom cabinet. Royal jelly. Freeze-dried blue algae. Powdered bitter melon. My lone bottle of multi-vitamins was outnumbered.

But that was before. These days there's barely enough money to cover bags of pasta and rice and beans—three foods that were formerly banned from our kitchen as not being paleo or not being keto or not being Whole 360.

Forget the supplements. We haven't had a jar of artisanal mustard or pickled artichokes in the house since March.

I don't miss the artichokes, but I liked that Dusseldorf mustard we used to get at the corner deli. It was great on ham.

I miss ham too. The pork processing plants were the first to close, and a lot of them never re-opened. The chickens went next. When you can get meat, it costs more than a bottle of Chateau Lafite. Tuna fish is still pretty cheap, but what's tuna fish salad without hard-boiled eggs?

Our local supermarket stopped selling eggs by the dozen and only offers them four at a time if you've got the money. We didn't even bother to stand in line for eggs, even when they were available. For the price of a third of a carton of eggs, you could buy a loaf of bread, a can of soup, and an apple.

In the early days of the lockdown, eggs, sugar, butter, and flour were sometimes hard to find, but that didn't keep people—including Rena—from baking. She baked all the time. Muffins for breakfast, brownies for lunch, cupcakes for dinner. At first the muffins were gluten-free and sweetened with applesauce or honey and the brownies were enriched with avocado puree and the cupcakes were vegan.

By June, though, she'd added cheese and bacon biscuits to the rotation and was covering the brownies with gooey caramel sauce and slathering the cupcakes with cream cheese frosting, negating a decade of sugar-free, dairy-free living.

But the bakery train came to a sudden stop in August when Rena got a note from her former employer saying the yoga studio where she'd worked had been evicted for non-payment of rent—the money had gone to covering the three instructors' salaries—and wouldn't be reopening any time soon.

Hard to social distance in a tiny yoga space tucked into a mini-mall.

"Maybe you could teach from home," I suggested. "Make a little money that way."

Rena had freaked out then, reminding me of how many celebrities were offering free yoga classes, exercise workouts, and daily motivation prompts.

"I can't compete with Omstars," she said. "Who's going to follow me when they've got Chris Hemsworth's fitness app?"

She had a point there. Even if somehow the yoga place did open back up, she'd eaten so much crap during the early months of the lockdown that she couldn't fit into her yoga pants anymore, much less manage and hold the *Taraksvasana*.

She used to be so flexible and bendy it was like having sex with an octopus. But after quarantine eating her stomach poked out more than her boobs, and the skin was stretched so tight over her fat belly that it was like balancing on a beach ball.

Not that I can talk. Once Rena started baking and opened the door to cheap meals like pancakes, macaroni and cheese, and potatoes fried up with onions and green peppers, I blimped up like a North Korean dictator.

I'd always worked at home, but that work had dried up for me during the late spring—it's hard to maintain social distancing when you're slobbing some guy's knob—and by fall it was clear the future of porn was with the amateurs uploading their solo efforts.

I'd approached Rena about filming her for the chubby chaser market, which is bigger than you think—but she said no.

Well, actually, what she said was, "Fuck no," so I took that as a no.

I'd always had a side hustle editing wedding videos, but with people cancelling their weddings or holding them over Zoom, I was shit out of luck there, too.

Rena sold some of her clothes on Etsy and I advertised for work on Craigslist, but by fall we were living like Walter White in the pilot of *Breaking Bad*, which I'd binge-watched seventeen times until we couldn't pay our cable bill.

"Gig work," Rena said gloomily one night as we ate peanut butter sandwiches washed down with cans of off-brand cola. A lot of the groceries in our fridge were off-brand, house-brand, and generic. Before this year, I hadn't even known there were such things as plain wrap beer and generic cigarettes.

"We've joined the gig economy," she added when I didn't reply.

"Yes," I said, because it was true.

"I don't really have any skills," she said.

"You can bake," I said. "Maybe we could start an online baking business. I could build a website—"

"Everybody learned how to bake for themselves last spring," she said. "And besides, how would we get the stuff to the post office?"

She had a point. When the Covid-deniers began emerging from their lairs in May, we'd sold our car to one of them for the price of two stimulus checks, figuring we could go without transport for the time being—Rena's studio was walking distance—and use the money we usually paid in insurance to keep the household running. But without a car, shipping anything meant we'd have to venture outside in our masks and gloves.

The risk to reward ratio was not good.

I drank the rest of my soda.

"What about doing a GoFundMe?" Rena finally said.

"Everybody's doing that," I said, but then I thought. *Wait a minute.*

"No, wait a second, that's actually a good idea."

"Really?" she said, her face brightening. I realized it had been a while since I'd said anything nice to her.

"Most people set up GoFundMe campaigns because they can't pay off medical debt, but now that we have universal health care, most people tune out. So we just have to come up with an engaging narrative. We have to figure out a way to stand out from the thousands of people who've fallen on hard times."

"How many thousands?" Rena said. I ignored the question because I was on a roll.

"We have to make sure our story sounds worse than anything possible donors are going through."

Rena looked discouraged as she considered the odds. "Everybody thinks they're going through the worst time," she said, dismissing the fundraiser idea. "You want another sandwich?"

"Sure," I said.

The moment she turned away, I stabbed her in the neck with a dirty fork that had been sitting on the coffee table since the night before.

You'd think with all the free time she had on her hands Rena would have done a little housekeeping instead of spending her days watching reruns of *KUWTK* on YouTube.

Her blood splattered all over, but fortunately, we had laid in a good supply of bleach and Lysol before the supermarket shelves got completely pillaged, so cleaning up would not be a problem.

When Rena finally stopped thrashing, I rolled her in our shower curtain and left her in the bathtub while I figured out what to do next.

Crowdfunding was one option, and I was pretty sure I could come up with a heart-wrenching story about my girlfriend who was murdered while venturing out for toilet paper and how I didn't even have money to pay for her funeral. Maybe I'd say her dog was killed too. People like dogs.

But that was pre-corona thinking. That was the kind of thinking you'd expect from someone dependent on the gig economy.

I wanted something more long-term and reliable.

Something that would keep paying off even after the wider world opened up. And I had the perfect idea.

I'd have to go outside to make it happen, but when I did, I'd have PPE up the butt. Just like everybody else out there.

I wouldn't be leaving fingerprints.

I wouldn't be leaving DNA traces.

And good luck trying to identify me from a high-angle, low-rez security camera shot.

Fuck trying to convince people to help me out of the goodness of their hearts.

But offering them a link to a Vimeo On Demand site where they could watch me murder someone in real time? Every week? That's an idea that'll make me some money.

NOBODY GOES OUT ANYMORE

Katherine LE White

Even as a small child, Marcello knew there was danger outside: the constant fight between nature and civilization. The plants, wild animals, bacteria, and viruses constantly encroached on humanity. Out his window he could see the worker bot tending the garden in front of his block, keeping nature at bay, its metallic body glinting in the sunshine.

Marcello saw a person outside for the first time when he was four years old. The outdoor maintenance bot malfunctioned, got stuck while pruning a tree. The arm that was caught remained still; the other three mimicked trimming branches that no longer existed. It would try to turn to do another task, only to stop when it realized that it was stuck on the branch, then begin the same procedure over again.

A day later, a truck drove up. That was not surprising in and of itself, but people got out, into the open air, not setting up a chute between their vehicle and the front door, not wearing body suits the way people did in the movies. They didn't explode. They didn't fall to their knees and start coughing up blood. Their eyeballs didn't fall out. They wore cloth masks, the kind that doctors wore, over their mouths and noses, but otherwise they were completely normal people.

"I want to go outside," he announced to his parents when he saw the people outside.

"Excuse me?" his mother asked, looking up from her monitor as she worked.

"You can't go outside, little man," his father laughed.

"They are." Marcello pointed out of the window.

Getting up from their portable computers to see what he was pointing at, his mother sighed. "Finally. That bot was creeping me out."

"They're a different breed of people, Marcello," his father said. "They have a dangerous job. One you don't want, believe me."

***

"The COVID-19 virus, the last deadly pandemic to hit humanity, struck in 2020," the college professor droned on. Marcello took his notes, trying to pretend he was interested, but he wasn't. Most of what everyone knew about *The* Virus, as it was called, was a mix of fact and fiction. It was highly contagious. It was deadly. It was outside, which was why most of humanity didn't go out anymore. "Once the pathogen was contained, the Sihense Filter invented to ensure clean air, and drone delivery technology perfected, we were 99% protected from the virus and able to live the life we do today. Thank your great-grandparents for their sacrifices, my friends. They did not live your cushy life."

Marcello already knew at this point that he would never be able to go outside. Despite his mother's wishes, he had been tested as soon as he had finished high school. His father had been exactly correct. The people he'd seen when he was four had been a different breed of people—immune to COVID-19. "Asymptomatic carriers," the nurse explained. "If you are one, you have to live separately from the rest of the population, but you do get the privilege of being able to go outside." She smiled widely. "That means you can be a first responder, go into maintenance, construction."

In other words, thought Marcello, *be a hero.*

But he was not immune, so he had to settle for being a dispatcher for the first responders in the field.

***

"So, do you get to meet them?" Marcello's new wife, Shantelle, asked. She propped herself up on her elbow, her curly black hair flowing down her back and framing her face in the low light.

They had been able to meet twice before getting married. Whenever anyone left a building and entered a vehicle (all of which were run under strict state surveillance), a tube was hermetically sealed to the door of the house at one end and the door of the vehicle at the other end, allowing no outside atmosphere to enter either space. The passengers then exited or entered and went about their designated business. Marcello and Shantelle had an engagement meeting at a fancy restaurant. An impressive total of 24 people were in the building, and Marcello felt crushed by the number of bodies in such close quarters, despite the more than 30 feet between each of the parties and the six feet between the individuals within each party. It was the best meal and worst conversation of his life. He could barely hear what Shantelle was saying - they both had to yell - and the waiters all wore masks, which made them impossible to understand. He hoped that he didn't sound like that over the mic he talked in dispatch.

Each of them got to pick four additional people to attend their wedding, so there was a gathering of ten in their new house. Their jobs qualified them for a fifty-year-old place in the suburbs. They had three bedrooms, two baths, and a covered plexiglass porch with a grill, all refurbished as a wedding gift from the government. Any other improvements were theirs to make from then on. They were starting out in a sweet situation, since the decimation of the population from generations before had left an abundance of housing open for posterity.

Marcello shook his head. "Just because they don't catch it doesn't mean they don't have it," he explained.

"So, technically, all first responders and maintenance workers have the virus, they just don't get the symptoms?" Shantelle asked.

Marcello nodded. One of the things he liked about his wife was her intelligence. They had been picked for each other by the government, based on tests taken from childhood onward. He found her lovely to look at, nice to talk to, smart...what was there not to like?

"That means if a first responder comes into your home, everyone in the house can catch the virus," Shantelle deduced.

Marcello put his fingers to his lips. "Don't ever tell anyone that."

Her black eyes went wide. "I know a State secret!" She smiled from ear to ear.

"Seriously," he said, trying not to laugh. "Don't go telling people that. They don't put two and two together, and you don't need to do it for them."

"My lips are sealed."

He kissed them to make sure they were.

***

"This is 911; what is the nature of your emergency?" Marcello asked into his headset, sitting in his small office in his home during his work hours.

"My wife just went outside," said a wavering, elderly male voice.

"Your wife just went outside?" Marcello repeated slowly, as per protocol.

"Yes," he croaked.

"OK, remain calm, sir," Marcello replied soothingly.

He muted the old man for a moment, "Female outside without protection," he called through the dispatch, giving the coordinates on his screen and the name and ages of people living there. There was something very familiar about the numbers flashing at him.

"Got it, Marc," one of the responders said. "Do what you do best, buddy."

"Sir," Marcello asked the caller, "what's your name?"

"Aaron," he said.

"Aaron, are you outside?"

"No." The old man's voice cracked. "I closed the door as soon as I saw it was open. I...I was scared. I left her out there….with the virus..."

"It's all right, sir," Marcello took a deep breath. "You did the right thing. You cannot help anyone if you do not keep yourself safe."

"She's knocking to come back in," Aaron whispered. "What do I do?"

Marcello's stomach dropped. "Aaron. Aaron? Are you listening to me?"

"Yes."

"Do not open the door. Do you understand?"

"Yes." Aaron's voice sounded small and defeated. In the background, Marcello could hear, "Aaron? There is something wrong with the door; it won't open. Could you help me with this, please?"

"I want you to come away from the front door," Marcello said with authority. "Go into your hall bathroom. You have a hall bathroom, don't you?"

"I do." Sounds of Aaron shuffling down the hallway drifted through the headset. "I can still hear her."

"Listen to me," Marcello instructed. "Close the door to the bathroom."

"Marcello!" Shantelle shouted from the living room, her voice filled with panic.

His heart caught in his throat. His body was already on high alert with Aaron on the headset, and Shantelle calling his name in such a way literally stole his breath from his body. He jumped up from his seat and ran out of his office, not sure at all what it must have sounded like to Aaron on the other end.

"I'm closing the door the bathroom," Aaron said to him. "I can't hear her anymore."

Marcello came to the living room, Shantelle was standing at the front window, a look of horror on her face. He followed her gaze to a house two lots away on the opposite side of the street and saw an old woman outside in a flimsy shift nightgown, knocking on the front door. She was frail, her light brown skin hanging on her bones the same way the nightgown hung on her. The gardening bots in the yard trimmed the bushes and tended the flowers, paying her no mind at all. She moved along from the door to one of the side windows, her feet bare and her gait slow and shuffling.

"She's outside, Marcello," Shantelle whispered, not taking her eyes from the window.

"I just left her outside," Aaron said at the same time. "Marcello? Is that your name?"

"Yes, sir," Marcello answered, still staring at Aaron's wife across the street. "It is." *What's taking the medics so long?*

"She's knocking on the windows," he said.

"Please stay in the bathroom. It is too dangerous for you to let her back inside. She may very well be infected with the virus by now," Marcello told him.

Shantelle's wide eyes turned from the window to him, her mouth dropping open. "You're talking to them?" she mouthed.

Marcello nodded vigorously. *Where are the medics?* "Aaron, is there anyone else in the house with you?"

"No," he answered. "Our kids are all grown."

"You didn't want to live with any of them when you were old enough to do so?"

"We don't want to leave our home," Aaron told him. "We've lived here 57 years, since we were married."

"You didn't choose to have in-home care?" Marcello tried to keep his voice calm as he watched Aaron's wife of more than half a century wander from window to window, tapping on each one, seeking entrance.

"We declined when we became eligible."

"You declined?" he asked amicably. "How come?"

"We didn't need it," Aaron said.

Like hell, Marcello thought.

The sound of sirens became distinct in the distance and Marcello ran back to his office, logging onto his dispatch computer, which showed the medical van approaching the house and dispatch trying to contact him. "We're almost there, Marc. How is the old man doing?"

"He's alone in the house, kids grown up and gone, no in-home care," Marcello explained, putting Aaron on mute once again. "He's torn up about closing the door on his wife. I've got him holed up in the hallway bathroom so he can't see her."

"Good idea. He'll be coming with us anyway. At his age, he can't stay at the house alone, and he's already been exposed with the door being opened. How'd she get it open in the first place?"

"I have no idea, I'm just trying to keep him calm."

"We're here, you can sign off with him," the medic told him.

Switching back, Marcello said, "Aaron, do you hear the sirens? That's the medics. They've arrived to take care of you and your wife. They are going to have to come into the house to take care of you, all right?"

"But they're coming in from outside," Aaron said. "They'll have the virus on them."

"They are trained for this. This is what they do every day, Aaron. They'll take care of you. You can't stay there by yourself. You can open the door for them."

"But you told me not to open the door," Aaron said, his voice loud. Marcello could hear the medics banging in the background.

"It's all right to open it now."

"But the virus..."

He muted Aaron. "You're going to have to force entry," he told them.

"Dispatch advises force entry," the medic said over the line.

"What's dispatch still on the line with him for?" someone asked.

"Doing his job, numbnut," someone else answered. "Keeping the patient calm until we make contact."

"The patient is outside!"

"Dumbass noobs."

"We got a a job to do, fellas." A female voice came on the line, and Marcello felt a rush of relief. It was the medic chief on duty that night. He knew her well by reputation. "Marc advises you to break the door down."

"Aaron." Marcello turned his attention once again to the old man. "Your wife is in an ambulance. They are going to take good care of her. They will get her to a hospital, where all of the facilities she needs for the deadly virus will be available to her. And to you, too." The crash of the door breaking could be heard from both the headset background and from the outside of his house. "They're going to come get you now."

"You said not to open the door!" Aaron yelled, his voice wavering with age. "You said--" His voice was lost in unintelligible yelling. Clearly the phone he was using had dropped to the floor. Scuffling ensued. Marcello stayed on the line for a few moments before hanging up and heading to the living room to watch with Shantelle.

The medics ushered the old woman into an ambulance, and she went willingly, smiling at them and talking as they closed the doors of the metal truck on her. Many slow minutes later, out came Aaron, not so willingly, being carried by three medics and a police officer, who helped to strap him into a stretcher. Marcello could see him screaming, but couldn't hear the words, just the noise of yelling as it made its way through the tiny cracks in his dwellings. He could still hear the echoes of what Aaron had told him earlier: *You said not to open the door!* One of the officers waved at him, and he wondered if the officer knew who he was or if he was just waving to the neighbors to let them know everything was going to be all right.

"What's going to happen to them, Marcello?" Shantelle asked, leaning into him as the vehicles drove off. The maintenance bots in the yard continued with their duties as if nothing had happened, as if someone still lived there.

"They aren't going to come back," Marcello told her, turning from the window.

"Because of the virus?" she asked.

He shook his head. "Stupid people," he muttered.

"What?" She followed him to his office. "What is it?"

"They refused help," he told her, sitting back down. "They didn't want to leave their home, so they didn't move in with their kids. And they didn't accept in-home help. So that's what happened to them. Carted away in an ambulances, never to be heard from again." He wanted to be outside at that moment, driving a truck, talking to Aaron, cleaning up the house next door, anything. What good was it talking on a damned mike? He let out a grunt and then punched the wall next to his desk.

Shantelle jumped, then licked her lips nervously. "They're going to die from the virus, aren't they?" she asked with a finality in her voice, her head nodding.

He looked at her, not sure if she'd heard what he had just said. Then he sighed, his heart sinking into his stomach, and he fought the urge not to vomit. "Yeah, honey," he conceded, "they went outside. The virus will get them." *If not the virus, something else will.*

TEXT-DOOR NEIGHBORS

Kahn Brown Jr.

Friday, March 5th, 2021

Estelle - I need your touch. 5:15am

Alexander - And I need to touch you.

Estelle – He tried to have sex with me again last night, but I told him I had a headache, but honestly I was soaking wet thinking about you.

Alexander - Baby, I know you're married. You have to do what you have to do to keep the peace in your house. I don't like knowing he's touching you, but…

Estelle – But I want your touch, not his. Between him being home all the time, and having you right next door but not being able to have you, this quarantine is driving me crazy!

Alexander – From what I'm seeing on the news, I think they are going to try opening things up again soon. We gotta hang in there, baby.

Estelle – I don't think we'll ever be free again. This is the new normal. Just when we were starting to get a nice little routine going, this shit has to come along!

Alexander – You can't give up

Estelle – I know I can't. Honestly, I just need some lovin!

Alexander – Any old lovin?

Estelle – You always say that! Of course not! I need yours. We have to figure out something soon!

Alexander – We will.

Estelle – Shit! He's up and already bugging me about what's for dinner tonight. I have to go, baby.

Alexander – Ok. Are we meeting at the window tonight? 10ish?

Estelle – Yes, but I have to keep my robe on from now on. I will open it so you can see me, but he woke up and almost caught me last time.

Alexander – Promise?

Estelle – Yes! Gotta go.

Sunday, March 7th, 2021

Estelle – Baby 8:00pm

Alexander – Hey!

Estelle – What you doing tomorrow morning about 6:30?

Alexander – I'm a prisoner in my own home just like you, neighbor. Why? What's up?

Estelle – He has to go in to his job tomorrow to sign some paperwork. It won't take long, but it's a 30-minute drive both ways. We'll have at least an hour.

Alexander – But what about Jonathon?

Estelle – I'm gonna let him stay up later playing his video games. He'll still be asleep when I sneak over.

Alexander – You're so devious!

Estelle – What? You don't want to see me?

Alexander – Of course I do.

Estelle – Well, don't be like that. It's been almost 6 weeks. I need some lovin!

Alexander – Just any old lovin?

Estelle – Stop it!

Alexander – Lol, what do I get out of this?

Estelle – You get me, of course.

Alexander – Any way I want?

Estelle – We'll only have an hour, baby.

Alexander – And?

Estelle – You're not getting anal. We won't have that kind of time!

Alexander – No deal then…

Estelle – What!

Alexander – Just kidding, baby.

Estelle – You better be kidding! Gotta go, see you in the morning. Love!

Monday, March 8th, 2021

Estelle – He just left. Be there in a minute. 7:02am

Alexander – I just got out of the shower. Back door is unlocked.

Estelle – mmmmmh

Estelle – He's asking me what happened when he left this morning. 12:20pm

Alexander – Why?

Estelle – Because when he got back I was sound asleep. You put it on me, baby!

Alexander – lol!

Estelle – He knows good sex will lay me out. I mean to the point where I'm snoring and damn near nothing will wake me up.

Alexander – You're pitiful…

Estelle – When I got back, I could hardly walk, lol.

Alexander – Smh… You're going to get us busted, lol.

Estelle – How?

Alexander – Sounds like he knows you. Are you that predictable?

Estelle – Oh… I never looked at it that way.

Alexander – Well, I don't want my tires slit, lol. So mix it up a little.

Estelle – Ok, baby, I will. And Thank You!

Alexander – For?

Estelle – For cracking my back, lol!

Alexander – Anytime, baby!

Estelle – I wish!

Alexander – Lol! Okay, any opportunity!

***

Wednesday, March 24th, 2021

Estelle – Did you like the pictures I sent? 6:00am

Alexander - Loved them! I still think you lied to me about your age. You don't have a flaw on you!

Estelle - Nope, I really am 39.

Alexander - Going on 25.

Estelle - I'm glad you like how I look. He never compliments me.

Alexander - His loss, my gain.

Estelle - True, but doesn't mean I don't get tired of how he treats me. Like I'm just his personal servant. Do you ever see a time when we're legit? I mean a couple?

Alexander - Is that what you want? A regular relationship?

Estelle - Honestly, I thought I just wanted something exciting because my marriage was so boring, but the more I get to know you, the more I wonder if it's enough. Good lovin is one thing, but a relationship is what every woman wants in the end.

Alexander - You've had me thinking about it too, honestly. I've really fallen for you. Didn't see that coming at all.

Estelle - And why not? I'm the shit, lol!

Alexander - So I've learned, lol.

Estelle - I'd divorce him for you. Not trying to scare you away, but I would.

Alexander - And Jonathon?

Estelle - He loves his dad, but I think he can tell his mom's not happy. Plus, I think he'd love you if he got to know you, and I would never keep him from his dad.

Alexander - You've really been thinking about this, haven't you?

Estelle - Yes.

Alexander - We're talking about flipping all of our lives upside down. Not that it wouldn't be worth it.

Estelle - Do you mean that?

Alexander - Yes, baby.

Estelle - I'm coming over.

Alexander - What!

Estelle – I'm going to tell him I need some air and I want to go for a short walk. He'll watch Jonathon if I agree to take care of him tonight, lol.

Alexander – Oh…

Estelle – Just a hand job. He'll never get me again! I'm all yours, baby!

Alexander – Even that makes me jealous, lol

Estelle – I'm gonna go to the end of the block, then cut down the alley and come in through your garage. Even if he was looking he couldn't see me from that angle. I need you to say what you texted to my face, plus I need to taste you!

Alexander – garage door is unlocked.

Tuesday March 30th 2021

Estelle – Baby! 10:00am

Alexander – You ok?

Estelle – I'm fine, but there's something wrong with him!

Alexander - How so?

Estelle - Well, he got a call from his job yesterday, and ever since he's been moody. Snapping at me and Jonathon.

Alexander - Did they lay him off?

Estelle - No, he's the head of his department. They're all working from home, but he's got job security in his position.

Alexander - I'm sure it's nothing major. Just workplace drama. Don't panic about it just yet.

Estelle - I couldn't take it anymore. I asked him what was wrong. 8:24pm

Alexander - What did he say?

Estelle - I'm scared, baby!

Alexander - What's going on?

Estelle - It seems that someone at his job has tested positive for the virus.

Alexander - But he works from home. Shouldn't be a problem.

Estelle – But, remember, he went in to sign some paperwork a couple weeks ago. The infected person was there too!

Alexander – Oh!

Estelle – Now the company says everyone who came in that day needs to be tested. What if he has it? What if Jonathon and I have it?

Alexander – I'm sure it's just a safety precaution. Has he felt sick? Have you or Jonathan felt sick?

Estelle – No, but it still scares me. I just want this all to be over. I want life to get back to normal. I want a divorce, but I don't want him to die. I'm not like that!

Alexander – I know you aren't, baby. Just stay calm and I promise you everything will work out just fine. I promise!

Estelle – He goes to take his test in about an hour. Can I call you then?

Alexander – Of course.

Monday April 5th, 2021

Estelle - Baby He has it! 6:47pm

Alexander - Shit! Now what?

Estelle - Well, he has no symptoms, but to be safe, they want me and Jonathon to come in to get tested. We both feel fine, but they want us to go just to be sure.

Alexander - Keep me posted, baby.

Estelle - I will, baby! I hope this isn't gonna scare you away from me?

Alexander - I promise you it won't.

Thursday April 8th, 2021

Estelle - Baby 10:10am

Alexander - Did your results come in?

Estelle - We were both positive, but they think we are going to be fine. No real symptoms to speak of. Apparently our immune systems are handling it pretty well.

Alexander - I'm in the ER, baby.

Estelle - What!

Alexander – I woke up during the night and couldn't breathe. I barely made it here.

Estelle – Oh, baby!

Alexander – I'm waiting to be seen, but from the way they are whispering around me and putting me in isolation, it doesn't look good.

Estelle – What hospital? I'm coming to you!

Alexander – You can't do that, and even if you could, they wouldn't let you in. Covid-19 patients aren't allowed any visitors.

Estelle – I'm so sorry, baby!

Alexander – Don't be. I'm sure I'll be fine. Apparently my immune system just isn't as strong as yours. But I'm sure I'll be back home soon. I love you. The doctor is coming in. Gotta go!

Friday April 9th, 2021

Estelle – Baby 3:14pm

Estelle – Baby 10:12pm

Estelle – You ok, baby? 11:53pm

Saturday, April 10TH, 2021

Estelle – Alexander, are you all right? 6:47am

CO(VENGEANCE)19

Rhashaa Price

Lenora went through her usual routine of cleaning the multimillion-dollar megachurch's building. The only thing different nowadays was the lack of people bustling through and around the hallways and offices. There were no children running and making what she'd once thought was too loud a noise, though on the contrary she'd now hear it as a welcoming sound. It had been six months since martial law had been lifted. It had taken people more time to trust coming out than it had for them to learn to stay inside.

The resistance to being locked in their homes, especially among the young, had been devastating. What's more, the weather had never really warmed up enough to help ward off the disease. It wasn't cold enough, either, to keep the crowd who saw themselves as invincible from trying to gather in secret places using encrypted messages through social media.

To Lenora, this seemed to offend the disease enough so that it mutated. As if 'it' was going to show humans who was more invincible. However, Lenora and others - especially health officials - tended to notice a slight bias in the pattern of infection.

Thus, Lenora and the others whom their community considered 'awake' believed that martial law was established not only to maintain control of the increase in the disease's spreading, but also to understand why some people were affected more than others.

Lenora pushed her garbage can around effortlessly for lack of weight from garbage. Trash was minimal. The echo of the rough wheels vibrated through the halls, making her feel lonely, but she knew these events were for the greater good.

She thumbed through her cell to glance at the email that came through.

"God , the Master, says: Because Edom reacted against the people of Judah in spiteful revenge and was so criminally vengeful against them, therefore I, God , the Master, will oppose Edom and kill the lot of them, people and animals both. I'll waste it – corpses stretched from Teman to Dedan. I'll use my people Israel to bring my vengeance down on Edom. My wrath will fuel their action. And they'll realize it's my vengeance. Decree of God the Master."

'WE WILL BE AVENGED!'

A twang of guilt came and left just as quickly. Lenora knew this to be truth for these times. She was glad she was one of the ones not to be affected, so far, by this pandemic.

***

Lindzey Ashley sat at her computer reading the latest email coming in from the superintendent of the public schools. She sat in awe of how slowly things were progressing with the lift. She had to admit, civil servants, those in the medical field, branches of defense, and science department were life-savers and heroes, but teachers also were to be given credit. Schools were closed, but teachers were still being paid to save the future by conducting online classrooms. Even after 9 months since the martial law being declared on account of the pandemic, not as many students were connected as should have been.

Lindzey pondered how long it might be before a functioning 'new norm' would be established so, selfishly, she could get her students back. How long? was the million-dollar question.

When the teachers were forced to submit final grades for their students due to the governor cancelling the school semester altogether, that event put things in perspective for Lindzey and her colleagues, as well as the students and their families. She ran a tally of all the children she knew would probably suffer during this time where school was their only norm in their little lives. Some of them looked forward to coming to school to escape the horrid environments they'd inherited at birth. Mental, emotional, verbal, and even sexual abuse was their lot in life, and their sanctuary was in an institutionalized education system.

Lindzey thought about at least one student she was making progress with despite their challenges. Rosia was a foster child who had been transferred from home to home because of the severity of her crisis. She and her little brother were molested by their mother and sold out to "tricks" for drugs and free rent. Rosia was finally getting the services she needed to deal with the various triggers that haunted her mind even at the so-called "safe-haven" of school. She dealt with peer pressure, bullying and being bullied, protecting her brother by being the mom from school life as well as foster home life. Somehow, Rosia trusted Ms. Ashley. Ms. Ashley was the one other teachers brought her to when she needed a buddy after several discipline issues. This made the "Shero" teacher happy and sad. Happy for obvious reasons. Sad because she knew not every teacher was innately blessed with discernment and patience.

Now, it was killing her wondering how the kids were doing through this. Even now that martial law was lifted, she'd seen neither hide or hair of Rosia or some other students.

***

"Hey Lenora, how's it looking over there?" Lindzey asked as she watched the news. Governor Holcomb had just announced that the evolved strain seemed to be losing its grip on society and the curve was beginning to flatten out, but the toll of death had a definite impact. The census was being reissued to try to get approximate numbers of who was left and how the numbers were changing.

"It's eerily quiet over here. They let me go a couple of days ago. There is nothing to clean. No one wants to come back," Lenora replied solemnly. "I see the numbers around the state have definitely increased. When I encounter some people, they look at me funny."

"Don't mistake that for a 'funny' look, girl. That is amazement, envy, and possible hatred."

Both ladies knew it was the truth. Social Media put out a few caricatures and memes showing people of color having super-human genes capable of triumphing over COVID-19. This caused a lot of 'clap-back' from various hate groups and individuals.

Conspiracy Theorist and people with more popular credentials had warned that this would be so: that fear would lead to desperation, especially among white supremacists, eugenicists, and such who had taken note of their leader, #45. The lifting of the ban and the apparent containment of the disease didn't guarantee safety for survivors. The conspiracy theorists on both sides and those on the borderline added fuel to the fire about why only people who lacked melanin were being afflicted.

"Linz? Are you protected?"

"Yes. I never thought in my life I would have to get one, let alone stock up. I just keep thinking about the children."

"Yeah. I'm glad I don't have any, even if it they would be safe...from the disease, I mean."

"I'll check on you later," Lenora stated as she bade goodbye to her sister.

***

"Because you kept my Word in passionate patience, I'll keep you safe in the time of testing that will be here soon, and all over the earth, every man, woman, and child put to the test."
Revelation 3:10 MSG

"The children have to be tested too?" Lenora questioned as she read one of the many emails that came through.

Lenora ended her call with a smile and redialed using the picture contact lists. Lindzey was on her favorites.

"Hey, I just wanted to let you know that there is hope." Lenora gleamed.

"How so?"

"Well, I talked to my friend Bridgette. Remember her? She is in the social work business."

"Yeah," Lindsey stated with a little more interest.

"She let me know that their department had worked it out so they can still get their time in with the children without going to the homes. They are doing virtual visits! She said it has made it more challenging for the foster parents and guardians because they must schedule these types of visits with all the service providers. Some of these kids have special needs, like physical therapy and all. If they have multiple kids…wow. But, nevertheless, they are still being checked on. Maybe this will give you some solace about some of your children," Lenora concluded.

"Yes, it has. Thanks, Sis."

Lindzey watched her daughter read her assigned book for their routine home-schooling hour. She adored her daughter as any parent would. During the time where biracial relationships were beginning to have a small level of acceptance, Lindzey felt blessed and cursed at the same time.

She was resolved that her daughter would survive because she carried her genes. But what if she didn't? The other side of the gene pool was being eliminated due to this pandemic.

More studies were being done to figure out what was the driving force that affected one race and not the other.

The news reported the shiftiness of scientists at Boston State University and said they have been brought to justice a few months ago. But now what? They should be made to work to cure this thing under strict scrutiny of the government.

As for Lindzey and her sister, Lenora, they felt protected, but they too had a fifty-fifty chance.

***

"Mom is sick!" Lindzey informed her sister.

"Man!" Lenora exhaled as she sat down to steady herself.

"We can't see her. Dad took her to the emergency room and then he was tested and sent away."

The soberness sank in deep between the sisters. Both shared tears through the cellular waves that kept them connected.

"I'm coming over. I gonna stay with you guys," Lenora said.

"Ok. I will get things ready. You think Dad will come?" Lindzey asked with much doubt.

"I already asked. He is taking it very hard. He won't," Lenora stated. She sighed. "He is afraid he will infect us and niecey-poo. He knows he will be ok, but he doesn't have it in him to take all the precautions to disinfect everything. And besides, he wants to stay where he is surrounded by things that comfort him about Mom."

"Well I guess it will be just the three of us", Lindzey said, feeling the sadness of that, but also comforted by knowing she would have the two most important people in her life close.

As they ended their call, another notification pinged on their phones. Lenora stared at it with trepidation.

Lindzey decided to read hers after preparing for the additional guest coming to set up camp.

"You will not fear the terror of night, not the arrow that flies by day, nor the pestilence that stalks in the darkness, not the plague that destroys at midday.

A thousand may fall at your side, ten thousand at your right hand, but it will not come near you. You will only observe with your eyes and see the punishment of the wicked." Psalms 91: 5-8 (NIV)

***

"This is Cybal Shyner of Channel 15 News. Although the curve has flattened and the White House announced some relief from COVID-19, they report that proactive precautions are still required to prevent a flareup or an unforeseen evolution of the strain appearing. CDC has developed trajectory data that clarifies, 'we have flattened out, but not snuffed out, this disease.'

"The president has given approval to continue administering the hydroxychloroquine treatment which has not proven to be 100% effective. Questions about the side effects, which include arrhythmia which causes heart attacks, vison loss, and psychosis, have been thwarted by evasive answers from the White House."

"Gosh, THAT MAN!" Lenora huffed out.

"Hey Lee, look at this!" Lindzey turned from her laptop so her sister could read along.

"The ACE2 gene is an enzyme that attaches to the outer surface of cells in the lungs and heart, and acts as a receptor for human coronavirus."

"What does that mean?" Lenora asked.

"It means we all have this gene. But look, this article states that it is more susceptible in some races than others!"

"Look, you took some medical classes. Think!" Lindzey was incredulous at how ignorant her sister was acting. "Read." Lindzey got up and paced the floor. "We had it all wrong! We had it all wrong!"

After a few minutes of searching, clicking, and reading on the computer, Lenora turned to her sister, staring and blinking with a ghostly look.

They both looked at Lizzy, and teared up, holding each other, watching as she played on the living room floor, engrossed in putting a puzzle together.

"Lord, she has to have a chance. She has to!" Lindzey whined as she slipped back into a chair.

The ping that came across their phones and computer cause them both to jump and look painfully at their devices.

"You live in the midst of deception; in their deceit they refuse to acknowledge me…Their tongue is a deadly arrow; it speaks deceitfully…Should I not punish them for this?' declares the Lord." Jer.9: 6-9

The ring from Lenora's phone nearly took them over the edge.

"Hey, sweety. How are you all?" the tired, gruff voice exhaled.

"Dad!" Lenora almost shouted the way she had as a little girl when she felt her dad was coming to her rescue.

Lindzey moved in closer. Leonora put the speaker on but turned the volume down. They both leaned in.

"Dad, remember the emails I said we have been getting?"

Silence. Just a ragged inhale.

"I don't think they were for us." The sisters leaned in, straining to hear anything their hero dad might say to relieve them of the panic embedded in their souls.

"Dad?"

"Your mom's gone. They…wouldn't let me…see her! I don't know where she is!" he said in between sniffs.

The stunned silence between the two sisters turned into whimpering cries. Lindzey glanced toward the living room to make sure the sounds of sadness did not reach her daughter's ears.

"Yes. I know about the emails. They were sent to me as well," Dad managed to squeeze out. "My daughters, you are in danger. They thought, since I'm white, you also were pure white. The information was false, and they are coming."

The sisters sat wide eyed. Their hearts seem to beat an ancestral drumbeat for survival.

"Listen, they just announced they are sending out buses to administer this crazy vaccine. You either take it or get boarded on the bus. Where they will take you isn't known, only theorists speculate you'll be taken toward Mexico, where the border wall project has been in effect all this time."

Sister silence.

"Look, I'm coming over there and I'm bringing supplies. They will do this strategically, so we have time to get ready. Check your supplies and GET READY!"

"We must leave our land because our houses are in ruins." Jer. 9:19b

CAN'T HEAL THE SICK

Josh Carson

Jackie and Brian talked about animal attacks during lunch. They had both seen a news program about coyotes in city parks, interviews with attack victims and mothers whose children disappeared. As they pulled out of a parking lot after eating, a coyote trotted casually down the sidewalk in front of them.

"Those things really are the worst offenders," Jackie said, flipping on the siren as she turned onto the street. "In Manhattan they've started crawling into windows and up fire escapes. They smell the bodies."

Brian closed his eyes and released a deep breath. She forced herself to smile so broadly that it changed her tone of voice. "Have you been to a house with animals yet?"

"Alligators."

"Alligators are rough. They're easy to shoot,

though." The siren blared despite there being no traffic. Jackie still used it to maintain some sense of control. She had been working emergency response in Miami since before the Sick Summer and had survived two bouts with the virus during unyielding service. She was given a medal she didn't care about and pawned it off to a dealer who specialized in buying medals from service workers. Her daughter needed rent. The siren was her favorite song. It was her anthem. It was the only sense of security she had left, and it was never going anywhere. The siren was home.

Brian thought it was unnecessary. His focus shattered every time the wail came back around. Jackie had taught him to breathe deeply, which helped. Reverence for people like her helped even more. He'd grown up watching all the movies and shows about the "essentials" and had decided early on that it was work too essential not to pursue. He 'd sworn an oath for people like Jackie. He owed her everything.

"So what's next?"

"I think..." she said, leaning forward and pulling down her sunglasses to peer over the top, "...that's..." she went on with a nod as her finger tapped the windshield near the middle where a dirty ten-story building towered over the surrounding strip mall, "...it."

Brian glanced down at the console in the dashboard. On target. "I hate hotels."

"It's a crapshoot, really. Big relief or the worst part of your week."

"I've only been to a few."

"One is enough. Everyone should see at least one." She nodded ahead. "This is a big one, too. A nine-to-fiver."

"Floors?"

"Eight-hour job."

Brian hunched forward under the windshield and watched the building get bigger as they got closer. It was slathered with shadows even under the afternoon sun, as though the sky wanted nothing to do with it. "Says 15 floors."

"It was open during the second wave."

Brian looked out the side window as Jackie scrolled through information. Houses were hollow, 1200-square-foot caskets lining empty suburban roads. Coded messages were marked on the doors so people could tell from a glance if they had been checked yet. He had learned how to read the messages in training from video footage of a hurricane's aftermath.

Pulling up, they saw that the hotel was so thick with moss it looked like an abandoned tower. Brian craned his neck out the window to get a better look while Jackie called in an initial report.

"3:19 PM, October 10th, 2031. Beachview Hotel. Off Coral Street. First eyes. It's a big one. Set check-in for fifteen, request security if backup is sent out." She sent it through. Her phone dinged when it was delivered.

"All right," Jackie said as she slipped on her mask. "Obituaries don't write themselves."

The first few times society shut down because of the virus, things didn't look so bad. Ghost towns. Lonely streets. Paranoia. The last time, people dropped dead all at once and environments were left in stasis. It took months to get around even the outskirts of cities. Metro centers were the last to be sanitized.

Three years had left the hotel in a functional state of dilapidation. Food had been raided and registers had been overturned by people who thought money still mattered even when nobody was alive to take it. The air was thick with stagnant humidity, as it had been during the last three increasingly warm springs and summers. Rotted overgrowth coated the baseboards and mold was caked into the carpet. Mushrooms were bunched up in corners and under overturned furniture.

Flashlights were almost pointless, their beams devoured by the shadows that sank into each hallway. The fungus was thicker underfoot in the dark, damp recesses, and the smell became so bad that Brian started to gag under the mask.

"Don't throw up in there," Jackie advised. "We're not going outside for you to clean it."

They checked every room. The doors opened easily with a master key. Most of the rooms on the first floor were vacant. They made marks on every door behind which a victim was found, and took notes. They moved on to the second floor, waving through the ivy and insects that flourished in the stairwell.

The second floor was worse. The mushrooms were so thick they audibly squished with every step. More of the rooms were occupied. Lots of children. Jackie let Brian cry when they found a child dead of starvation curled up next to a parent dead from the disease. She wished she could still cry like that.

"They don't pay us enough for this," was the only solace she could think to offer.

After that, she let him record info and mark doors while she took over room searches. She was in one of the last rooms on the wing when Brian moved past the rusted elevators and danced his light down the hall. He almost ran into Jackie as he returned. "There's no fungus."

"Don't wander off." She squinted. "Where? Down the hall?"

He took her past the elevators, and they both looked down at rotten carpets peppered with the stems of plucked mushrooms.

"Who would pick these? Are they even edible?" Jackie turned towards the elevators. Brian kept his attention on the hall. "Brian." She turned, waving her flashlight at him. "Brian!"

He turned to answer her but saw what she was calling to his attention to before he spoke. The elevator doors had been pulled apart by bare hands which left massive dents on both sides where the doors meet. One of the panels was caved in and wedged in the track. Jackie looked into the shaft, moving her light up and down.

Brian tried to peer in around her. Then he turned and looked behind them. "Did rioters do this?"

"No," she said, her voice echoing up and down the shaft. Jackie pulled her head out of and inspected the dent. She put her hand inside and frowned. Ridges? "Brian." She angled the light for a clearer view.

Knuckles. "Brian." He was holding onto the door wedged in the track, leaning in to look up. "It's a punch."

He got out half a shout before crashing to the floor. The rest came out in a mewling sob as he was shoved into the open shaft. Jackie shouted and sprang to the elevator, screaming his name through the doors.

Then she heard the noise.

At first she thought it was a dog behind her. Then she thought it was a bird above her. When she looked up, a shaggy head pulled itself from the shaft back onto one of the top floors, launching a deep-throated hack that erupted into a shrill cackle. The sound by itself felt like an assault, and she pushed herself away from the door moments before a slab of concrete dropped.

She thought of Brian and rubbed the back of her head. The concrete. She took a deep breath to gather her thoughts and considered which end of the hall was a better exit option.

A bark bounced through the elevator shaft behind her. She turned slowly, clicking her light off when she let herself process that the response came from the first floor.

She launched herself down the hallway without mushrooms, keeping one hand along the wall, sliding as she went to touch every doorknob. She kept her eyes forward, running fingers across the braille to make out numbers she half-remembered from a seminar.

Ahead of her she heard a latch being wrenched. She stopped. A door churned open. She immediately pushed on the door next to her, hoping to open it. Her heart sank heavily when she remembered that Brian had the key.

When the door slammed she knew something was coming down the hall in front of her. She shuffled back, staring alertly into the pitch dark. Single knocks came at intervals. Someone –something--was rapping at every door, one after another, steadily drawing closer. Deciding whether to hide in the elevators or sprint for the other end of the hall in hopes that it was clear for escape was terribly difficult. The knocking made her want to run. The thought of being trapped in the hall made the idea of running that way intolerable.

She went to the last room she had inspected for bodies, pushed the door open all the way, muttered a prayer to nothing in particular, and sprinted to the elevator. She knew how long the doors took to shut, so she knew how long she had before a noise, and she pushed everything out of her mind so there was no doubt when she slid through the broken elevator doors and gripped the hanging cables.

The door in the hallway shut. The knocking went wild from the other end.

She lowered herself, grimacing under the strain when her arms started searing. The riot-control exercises at her job's boot camp required scaling rope, but who had time to visit the gym when so many 10-hour shifts had to be covered?

Her arms were shaking, her shoulders popping as they stretched. She swung one foot wildly to push herself against the wall under the doors, scraping her fingers to cling onto tiny cracks, desperately trying not to be seen. She looked down, judging the distance if she fell. Brian was crumpled in a splatter of blood in the basement at the bottom of the shaft. At least twenty feet.

Whatever was coming down the hall stopped at the elevators. She could hear heavy snorting breaths like a horse's, soaking wet coughs breaking into a growl that sounded like a person pretending to be a cat. The knocks became slaps, pounding the doors. The steps became stomps, like galoshes smashing wet mushrooms into puddles. Barking exploded again, angry hacks from the back of a throat. Jackie closed her eyes. The sound was so visceral it made her feel pictures.

She heard the door to the room opening. Something stomped around inside. She heard faint crashes before it opened again and another frustrated rumble ripped through the hall.

When the smell finally reached her she started to realize what was hunting her. A rancid mix of a skunk, mildew, shit, and wet garbage, like a stray dog that had drowned in a sewer during the summer. Most people knew those beasts by their smell. There was no other like it. Chimps and apes had escaped from cheap tourist traps around the Everglades and interbred in filthy isolation. Fifty years of genetics had spiraled into a natural abomination: the swamp ape.

Listening as it moved back into the hall, screeching and pounding on walls, she could visualize it clearly. The multi-jointed arms, the stubby legs, the drooling jowls and glassy eyes. The matted hair, the off-sized fingers, the hands as big as dinner plates. Dragging bloody knuckles. They could walk, but they chose not to.

Some of the swamp ape victims she'd seen had no heads. Some had heads that were flat in the middle, crushed from both sides. Some had lost arms or legs. Most were recorded as accidents or mishaps. "Florida Men" were actually mutant beasts that dwelt in foul waters.

She looked up, plastered to the side of the elevator shaft, expecting to see the head watching her from high above, terrified that it would pop back out the moment she swung to the middle.

She looked down. The bloodstain was uncovered. Brian's body was gone. Glancing back up, she tightened her grip on the cables, dropped from the side, and inched down. She lowered herself, keeping close watch above.

She was almost to the first floor when shouting came thundering through the lobby. The backup she had suggested rushed the place with a harsh shout of "FREEZE," catching her heart between fear and hope. Guns fired. She clung tighter to the cable until they stopped. There was a silence, but it wasn't cold and frightening anymore – it felt warm and secure. She was about to call out when somebody said, "What the fuck?" and the guns went off again.

Then they stopped for good. Absolute chaos erupted. Panic-thickened voices fell into screams. Jackie shook her head, closed her eyes, muttered prayers she didn't even believe in herself, and winced harder and harder every time somebody's desperate cry for mercy drowned in violent death rattles.

The next silence was not warm. She wrapped herself around the cables, counting to 10,000 before continuing down to leave. She choked on her number when she felt herself starting to rise. Above her, massive hands tugged the cable while a shaggy head watched. The arrested flight-or-fight response burned fear from behind her heart all the way into her gut. She vomited in her mask as she was pulled to the top.

She saw that her captors were not apes. Apes had real eyes, a specific facial structure, four fingers on each hand, and hair kept groomed. They walked on their knuckles. The creatures who surrounded Jackie had shark eyes, variably misshapen skulls, and what could technically be considered thumbs. Their hair was thick and rancid, crawling with bugs that made nests in the tangles. They were close to her height when they crouched over on their fists. When they held themselves like men, she had to look up.

Not that she did. She averted her eyes when they grabbed her by her arm and pulled her onto the top floor. Her shoulder dislocated, which made her yell out without thinking. They mimicked her cries until she managed to roll it back into place. Then they gathered around her, blocking her view past their circle, watching her writhe. When she looked up at what would be considered their faces, she felt that each one of them had the same pair of eyes.

She looked down again. Most animals took eye contact as a challenge. Were these animals? They sounded and moved like them. Were they people? The way they looked at each other and communicated made her feel as if she was surrounded by humans whose language she didn't know.

One of them nodded and the circle dispersed. She kept her eyes down, unsure whether their civility was more or less comforting than their overt hostility. The one who had nodded rose to its full height and reached over to push her forward with a big hand. The rest of them moved back, spreading through the wide-open space they had made by demolishing barriers across the entire floor. There were dozens of the creatures. She looked at the tall one. It was staring silently away, waiting for her to follow its gaze.

Bodies were stuck along the wall, tied or nailed with crude irons. They were indistinct at her first glance, which she tried to make her last, but the tall one kept her facing the carnage until history started to take shape across the gruesome diorama.

Most of the bodies were dead from disease, decayed, bits of spongy flesh left like tufts on dry bones and infection caked to their ribs. They were dressed. At the near end of the display a few were pinned together, cups and containers and cigarette butts and other garbage accessorizing each corpse. One of them had sunglasses on. One had a phone tied to their hand.

One of them was positioned as if they were coughing.

The bodies started to stack after that, first two, then three, and on and on until they were stuffed into a pile that wedged against the ceiling. The first wave.

The bodies were half active. Some sat, sipping from their soda cans. Some lay in heaps. Some were dressed and posed as doctors, some as workers and shoppers in grocery stores. These displays stretched the floor's length, wrapped around a far corner, and kept going until they eventually tapered off behind her, near the door. In some places people arranged to look as thought they were dying sprawled between piles of bodies. Jackie's captors had documented the pandemic.

She followed the display all the way. Scenes representing "survivors" grew fewer and farther between as it went on. She caught her breath when she reached a dead creature like her captors which was posed as though still eating a dead woman. Then the bodies of the swamp apes began to pile up. First they lay intermingled with the people, and then by themselves. As their pandemic was ravaging them, a homeless man must have taken refuge in their building. She knew this because he was dead on the wall, clothes stiff with blood, face half torn from his skull. She looked closer at the face. He'd died less than a year ago, maybe.

On the floor under him was Brian, blood still leaking, body contorted so unnaturally that Jackie felt dizzy looking at him. It took everything in her power not to drop to his side. His eyes were wide open. He was long gone. A security officer from the lobby was laid on top of him, head twisted half backwards, bone torn through his arm. One of his eyes was gone.

Beside them a creature was seething, pumping hot spit from behind its crooked jaw, blowing hot mist with every labored breath. Its hand clutched its shoulder, relaxing and tightening its grip rhythmically. She knew that wince. It must have been the one downstairs. It had been shot.

The room started to hum with snarling whispers. The tall creature was moving closer. Others closed in behind, their chattering meshing into a mangled chorus. Her gut dropped and her mind turned inside out. She was going on display.

She moved towards the creature who was wounded, prompting a rush from the group. The injured beast started to lash out at her, and she held out a hand, closed her eyes, and gave the last option her final shot.

"NO."

They stopped. There was howling from the back, and the tall one moved in on her quickly, but she kept perfectly still with her hand out and repeated the word in a much different tone.

"No."

Nothing moved. Jackie looked from the crowd of her captors, to the wounded beast, to the wall of bodies they had carefully arranged. She slowly moved towards the display, keeping her eye on the crowd, so desperate to communicate that she actually grabbed the arm of a corpse dressed like a doctor and shook it wildly as she patted her chest.

The tall one looked from her to the bleeding creature in the corner. It looked back at her and nodded.

She returned to the corner and dropped to her knees

beside the wounded creature. It snarled and howled but didn't fight her even a little as she dug two fingers into the gaping hole in its leathery chest.

***

They let her go after she pulled the bullet out. First they showed her a floor full of their own kind, sick and dying from the disease, coughing and gasping for air. She shook her head at them and tried to share a sympathetic look. She could pull a bullet out, but she couldn't heal the sick.

They weren't angry, but they had no more use for her. One of their children led her into the stairwell and flung the door open with an abrasive shriek before running away, chortling to itself like some hellspawn hyena. The stairwell was exhausting to navigate. The wet air drowned her lungs with toxic heat. Mosquitoes flew freely. She stepped on snakes and felt tiny bones crunch.

The lobby was empty except for a few deer that scattered when she came out from the stairs. She dutifully checked each of the members of the security team, although it was clear from how they were lying that none of them had survived. Two had arms pulled out of their sockets.

When Jackie got outside, another team was securing the area. She dropped her mask and took a deep breath, coughing out the stink of decay and vomit. A police officer helped her over to an ambulance while gathering some general information.

"How many bodies up on the top floor?"

Jackie had to guess. "Two hundred? Maybe two fifty?"

"And how many swamp apes?"

"Who knows?" She was staring hard at nothing. "Generations."

The officer whistled low. "I better get my boss down here. We're going to need more people, probably something from the army–"

"No," she said. "Just leave them alone. The disease is inside of them, too, they're coughing it around now. It'll take care of itself."

"What if we want to take care of them instead?"

"Because of what they did to our friends in there?"

"Yes, ma'am."

"Then let them die like we did."

ROUND ONE: MASK VS. NO MASK

Chris Rodriguez

"I'm not taking any chances this time." Mona packed an extra mask, her pepper spray, and eight rolls of state quarters in her shoulder bag. Since Billy lost his job at the factory she had scraped the bottom of *every* cookie jar in the house. The paper currency they had squirreled away was long gone, not that it was worth diddly squat. Food, gas, and supplies had skyrocketed in price. When the banks closed to reset the currency to digital blockchain (whatever the hell that meant) people were forced to trade in barter items when they ran out of cash.

Just the night before, Billy had helped her pin Little Bean down while she threatened their twelve-year-old son into giving up his coin collection. She swore the kid was a born-again Rockefeller the way wealth just flowed to him like a money magnet.

"Little Bean! I'm gonna let your sister lick your face right here and now if you don't give it up! This family has to stick together, help each other."

The cupboards were nearly bare, but she couldn't face sitting in her car for hours in a miles-long food line for the fortieth time only to be turned away by the National Guardsmen when the food ran out way too soon. She just didn't have the strength - or the gas. Plus, people were just plain angry. Short fuses just waiting to be lit. Mona didn't want to be anywhere nearby when the explosion came.

"No!" LB had struggled against the firm grip on his thin limbs. Billy was a small man, almost petite, but wiry and strong.

Grandma Grace, tiny but mean as a mongoose when riled, stepped up to where LB could see her tiny little tapestry house slippers. He could only open one eye while his face was being ground into the carpet.

"Little Bean," Grandma wheezed. She had caught the Rona two years ago, but somehow survived. It was a miracle! Truly. She had every risk factor ever listed for Covid-19 and she beat it. Now she was twice as powerful as anyone else on planet Earth. Like she'd risen from the dead!

"Don't make me, Grandma. Please! It's the only thing I have left."

"Little Bean," she warned again, "it's the only thing *we* have left."

LB gave in. "I sure as damn hell don't want my fat, ugly little sister lickin' her Covid-cooties all over my face."

Mona snickered. She wondered what his pandemic-traumatized mind was thinking might be living in Lulu's nasty mouth.

LB liberated the money from his secret hiding place. Mona heard him lock the door while he did it. She hoped something else would show up for him to hide in the future. She did feel badly about taking his treasure.

Mona was ready to go while it was bright and early. "Get in the car," she hollered. She stood by the open door while her family dutifully filed out. They climbed into their designated seats in the 2018 Dodge Journey Crossroad.

They had never had reason to use the off-road capability, but she and Billy had talked late at night sometimes about what to do if they needed to leave in a hurry. Billy had made good money at the plant as a floor manager, especially when he pulled double shifts or covered quality control. They'd been able to pay cash for the SUV two years ago. A family trip had been planned for a cross-country drive on Route 66. Never happened. The Coronavirus pandemic put their plans in lock-down.

Two years later, all they had was LB's quarters to get to a dollar store. The house was another matter. It was due to be foreclosed on within the month. She shook her head.

What in the world is a busted mortgage company going to do with yet another empty house? Nobody in this town could afford to buy it. None of it made sense to Mona.

All she was concerned about that day was feeding her family. They all peered out of dusty windows as they rolled through the once immaculately manicured neighborhood. Wide-eyed people heard the motor. They peeked through drapes and blinds to see who was near their homes. Nobody was out in the yards. They were afraid someone would ask them for something. Lawns were knee-high due to rationed fuel, bushes unpruned, and many windows covered with plywood just like their own. Garbage piled up on the curbs emitted the smell that helped keep people safe in their homes. City service had ended weeks ago when the strikes started.

"There they go," Billy said, pointing to the slow-prowling police unit. "What good are they?"

"I know, Billy," Mona said. "We've talked about this. After the protests, people wanted them defunded. They didn't realize the implications."

"Well, there was protests and there was something else. You know. We was there! Something evil about all that rioting." He pinched his lips together tight. "All they good for is taking back the stolen goods from those street punks." Billy was like a pit bull when it came to injustice. He wasn't going to let go. "Then they keep it all for themselves!"

He pulled up near the dollar store's front door. Although it was at least 30 minutes before opening time, a few other cars with families were parked there, waiting. Word spread fast whenever a store was open for business. Whole families crammed into vehicles. It wasn't safe to leave people unprotected at home.

"I'm going in by myself," Mona said. "It will be faster. You kids stay in the car."

The layout was familiar to her. She would grab a cart and get as much as she could with $80. In fact, she should be faster than she had been last time. Many pounds had melted off her since the pandemic started. A forced diet. She dragged her purse, weighted with a good extra four pounds, onto her lap. She was ready to get out and go as soon as she saw the clerk turn the key in the lock. No waiting lines allowed. She adjusted the mask, pinching it tight around her nose. No way did she want the new, improved mutation of this eternal virus. A new one circulated about every six months. The promised vaccines never worked against this chimera.

A yellow sign on the door said the store would be closing to restock on Saturday. Similar signs had been posted at many other stores. They never opened again – unless it was to sell used goods or a surplus of barter items more like a flea market.

A trip to another town to shop would use too much fuel. Anyway, the ongoing protests and riots had nearly burned them to the ground along with the good citizens' indignation. This time people were rioting because they were hungry and scared.

"Wish me luck," she said as she climbed out, quickly gauging the distance from the car to the store. She needed to be first in line to stay ahead to grab items that might be the last ever on the shelves. She replayed the game plan in her head, her mental map of top priority sections in the store. Food, of course, but she also needed to grab what was left of the toilet paper (or a reasonable substitute), and also any over-the-counter medicines that were still available. She thanked her lucky stars they didn't have a baby. Delmar, the youngest, was now four. Well past potty training and baby necessities.

The lock clicked on the double doors. She charged ahead, grabbing the door handle with one gloved hand. She was in!

Later, Mona checked her time. It had taken a good 20 minutes to fill her cart and get to the checkout stand. Not bad. She was second in line at the stand closest to the doors. There was the expected distance between her and the man in front. She took a deep breath and looked around. Everyone, as the posted notice ordered, was wearing a mask. Giddy with self-satisfaction, she was startled when there was a bump against her behind.

As she turned to see what the hell was going on, the lady behind her bumped her again with a cart even more full than Mona's.

"Move up!" the woman demanded. "Don't need to make me hang out in the aisle like this."

Oh, no, you didn't! Mona was livid. This rude woman who was violating her space wasn't even wearing a mask. Mona turned all the way around and slowly, deliberately, pushed the cart away from her body.

"Keep your distance, please," Mona said. "You're not wearing a mask."

The woman pushed back. "Get your gloved hands off my cart!" she cried. "Don't you be *touching* my stuff." She rammed the cart into Mona's stomach. "I have *rights*! I don't have to wear no suffocating mask."

At this point, Mona saw red. *What in Dante's hell was this woman doing? Didn't she know she was endangering lives?* She grabbed the woman's cart with her gloved left hand, took her handbag off the handle with her right and swung it all the way back, planning to smack that idiot right into the empty shelves in the paper goods aisle.

A crash brought Mona back to reality. She turned to see she had hit the man checking out behind her. The heavy bag filled with quarters had caused him to pinwheel backward, knocking over a display stand. The debris then blocked others from coming further into the store beyond the doors. Then she heard another crash. She spun back toward the woman.

The crazy unmasked lady had yanked the cart from Mona's hand so hard she had lost her balance. She fell into the man behind her. With no sturdy cart to distance himself, he was caught off guard and fell flat on his back.

"Look what you made me do," the woman screamed at Mona.

By this time the store stockers, the manager, and the two other register clerks had circled the warriors. With arms outspread, they readied themselves to jump in to hold one or the other back physically if necessary. One stocker helped both men up off the floor. Neither were injured, but the individual behind the unmaked woman slipped on the spilled dish soap from the bottle he had been holding and fell again, taking the stock clerk down with him. Both started swearing loudly.

Neither woman noticed what was going on around them. They were intensely focused on throwing knives from their flashing eyes. Neither was going to give in until someone died.

The nervous manager stood between them. "Ladies, could we just get things moving along here? You can finish your discussion outside." The stockers bustled around getting the display case upright. The trapped customers crammed into the tiny space against the doors were jostled when people outside tried to get in. "Get that cleared up!" the manager barked.

Mona glared one last time at the stupid woman who was rolling her eyes at the manager. She stepped up to the cash register. The man who had been in front finished checking out and decided to wait down by the middle register to stay clear of the confusion. The clerk price-checked Mona's items in record time. She helped Mona load the bags into her cart just as the display stand was placed upright. The small crowd moved freely down the aisles again. The doors were clear.

The red-faced manager stayed in place between the two women for a moment, then stepped away to escort the man who had knocked over the display stand. He didn't want lawsuits about his store. Not that there was a court open to process one.

Mona got all the way to the door before she heard, "You're just prejudiced. You think I'm gonna give you the virus 'cause I'm Black! You're probably one of those White Power people!" The woman spat the words out along with a fine spray of saliva, prompting the clerk to step back a couple of inches. The plastic shield fixed across the check stand caught the droplets.

Enough was enough. Mona raised her shoulders up almost to her hot pink ears. She opened the doors, pushed her cart out, and yelled for Little Bean to come load up the car, then turned and went back to the check stand where the lady who had accused her of this heinous crime stood waiting to leave. The bare-faced woman held on to her cart like a shield.

The good Lord Himself wouldn't have been able to stop Mona. She pulled the full cart from the woman's clenched fingers, reached over, grabbed the woman by her hair and dragged her to the open door.

"Do you see those brown kids out there?" Mona pulled the screaming woman's head up higher. "Those are *my* kids. Who do you think you are, talking to me like that? You don't know me!" Then she yelled, "Lulu! Stop pushing your little brother off the sidewalk! You want him to get hit by a car?" Then, "Billy, for crying out Pete sakes, can't you *watch* these kids for five minutes?"

The woman loosened Mona's fingers from her hair. She stood, mouth agape, staring at the kids climbing back into the SUV. Her eyes opened wide as she marched up to the driver's side.

"Billy Hartwell! That you?" She knocked on the window. Billy reluctantly rolled it down a few inches.

"Billy, it's me! Marilyn Sykes… well, Robinson now."

A slow smile stretched across Billy's face. "Marilyn? Why I haven't seen you for what, fifteen years? How you doin'?"

Mona stalked up behind the woman and glared at Billy. "What do you mean, 'How's she doing?' Don't you know what happened in that store?"

The two ignored her and kept on chatting away as if they were at a church social. When Billy rolled down the back window, the woman leaned in and said, "That you, Ms. H? How you been? You look *good*."

Grace barely glanced around. "I'm alive. Praise the Lord."

Mona couldn't stand it. "Billy, what the hell is going on here? Is this some kind of family reunion?"

Billy quickly explained. He and Marilyn's boyfriend had been best friends in high school. In fact, she had married Cornell. Billy hadn't seen his friend since his family moved from the old neighborhood.

"Listen," Marilyn-The-Unmasked said, "whyn't y'all come over tonight. We're having a get-together… a planning meeting with some of our friends. We need to find a better place. This town ain't safe." She turned her head to look at Mona.

Billy cocked his head at Mona in that cute puppy-dog way he had.

Mona's mouth dropped open in disbelief. *I can't believe this is happening!*

"Can't do it alone, Babe," he offered.

"I don't know." Mona still had her dander up. She didn't know this woman like Billy did. How could you trust someone who didn't play by the rules?

"Come on." Marilyn looked hopefully at Mona, then stuck out her hand. When she saw the way Mona looked at it, she drew it back, remembering it was no longer socially acceptable to shake hands.

Mona looked at Billy, then at Marilyn. She slipped her hand inside her handbag, then stood facing Marilyn full on with one hip cocked out to the side, her jaw cocked out to the other. She flipped the extra mask from her bag and held it out toward the unmasked woman.

Marilyn pursed her lips then laughed. "All right, Sugar. I'll wear a mask." She reached for the cloth dangling in Mona's hand. Mona moved it away from her reaching fingers. She set her jaw again.

"You're right. We'll *all* wear masks at the meeting. I'll see to it." She winked as Mona allowed her to take the mask. "Bring those water crackers you got," Marilyn added. "They were the last ones on the shelf."

They both smiled, then turned when footsteps came up behind them. A gang of boys who harassed shoppers had snuck up on them while they were distracted.

The two women turned to face the mob. They stepped together, standing shoulder to shoulder. Neither made a move to get into the safety of their cars. Marilyn's cart had been pushed through the doors behind her. She put one hand on it possessively and raised her chin high. Billy opened the door of the car; one leg slid out. Mona held her hand up to stop him. The door shut quietly. Her eyes never left the boys. Five stood tough, but no weapons flashed in their clenched fists.

"I don't guess you boys want to mess with us today," she said slipping the pepper spray out of her bag.

The boys glanced back and forth, assessing the situation. Mona gave them the same hard look she had given Marilyn, including the cocked hip and set jaw. Both crazy-looking women sported rumpled clothes. The boys checked out Marilyn's wild hair, her smudged lipstick.

"You see the mess inside the store? *We* responsible for that. Be glad to show you first-hand." Marilyn raised her painted eyebrows high.

The boys shuffled around for a minute; then the one in front narrowed his sky-blue eyes over the top of the grimy bandanna that covered his face. He tossed his blonde locks. "Vámonos!" he ordered. The others turned as ordered to slink back to the corner. An easier target would come along soon. "Next time," Blondie warned them.

The women started to high-five their victory, then switched to an elbow bump. Mona went to get into her passenger seat. Marilyn gave Billy contact information, then threw one last wave and left. The children had never been so still and quiet. Billy looked over at Mona, waiting for her to come around. He could see she was upset. A deadly rattler ready to strike, she took his hand and squeezed it firmly.

"It's a lot more difficult," she said, "to make new friends in this New Normal."

IT'S OKAY. YOU'RE IMMUNE

Veronica Smith

"You can save the world. You're immune." The voice taunts me in my dream as I see myself strapped to a bed, an IV inserted and taped to my arm. "You'll save millions of lives."

I struggle, trying to free myself from the straps, wanting so badly to rip the IV from my arm. The voice belongs to a doctor, completely encased in a white biohazard suit that crinkles when he walks. He looks at me, then quickly bolts for the door. Someone inside pushes a button, and he yanks it open. The door is closing, but not fast enough. I see the doctor double over, his body racked with coughing. He looks at me once more before the door finally shuts. Somehow, I can still hear coughing from beyond the door. He's not the only one coughing. What happens if they all die out there while I'm still trapped in here? What happens to me?

As weeks go on, I see fewer and fewer people, and all of them are sick. I begin to fear I'll never get out of here. Then, like a miracle, a young woman manages to get my door open. She props it open with a chair as a dry racking cough brings her to her knees. She stumbles to my bed and undoes the straps. I immediately yank the IVs out of my arm, my own blood dripping on the floor. The woman collapses on the floor and dies in the middle of a cough. After removing all the rest of the tubes, I flee.

***

The COVID pandemic hit the world in early 2020. It peaked several times, but once December rolled around it seemed it was winding down. By February 2021 everyone had gone back to their daily lives and forgotten all the precautions the government and doctors warned them to take. And for a few months it did appear that the virus had run its course. Until the summer of 2021. Then the end of the world began.

Doctors' worst fears were realized. The virus somehow merged with the bubonic plague. The plague had begun to pop up in remote areas of China and spread just enough for it to marry the COVID bug. While bubonic itself was treatable with antibiotics, the new improved version with a dash of COVID was incurable, and no one was safe, masked or not. The new virus was highly contact-contagious, and then it mutated and went airborne.

And so the BUB-COVID was born. The death rate was over 50% when the 2021 pandemic first started, but that quickly rose, and within less than a month of its reemergence the virus was killing 80% of the infected. And everyone was getting infected. Literally everyone. All too quickly the death rate rose to 99%. The only way to not get it was to never be exposed. But by then everyone had been exposed. No one lived in a bubble. Those that had locked themselves inside early on became infected when they finally came out for food, being forced to choose between contracting the virus and starving to death.

Somehow the CDC discovered a rarity: About one in every five million people was naturally immune. I was one of the lucky ones - or unlucky - depends on how you look at it.

I'd lost my four-year-old son to BUB-COVID. My husband and I mourned him and stayed locked up in the house, only going out when we needed food, unable to even have a funeral for our little boy. The rest of the world descended into chaos around us. The grocery stores were emptied despite the quantity restrictions. Toilet paper flew off the shelves just like it had when the pandemic first started. I wasn't a hoarder, but I had always bought a package here and there whenever it was on sale, so I just let them pile up, stacking them up in the spare bedroom. We ate as little as we could to make food last. Once the virus mutated and people started dropping dead in the streets, the stores were finally able to keep some essentials in stock. I think they had incoming deliveries for maybe a month before there was no one healthy enough to make deliveries. Hell, by then hardly anyone was even able to go out to get supplies. My husband got sick, but I didn't. That's when I realized my immunity.

He got sicker as each day passed, and he became so congested he could hardly breathe. We had no food left in the house, and I was running out of water. On the morning after I gave him the last of the cough syrup, I realized that I had to get supplies. I hated to leave him, but we couldn't live without food or water, even if he survived the virus. With tears in my eyes, I kissed him goodbye. He smiled and whispered, "I love you," before coughing again. I left the house with a gun in my pocket and my camphor-soaked mask on my face. That was the last time I ever saw him.

My car was full of gas. I hadn't driven it in the month since we last dared to shop. I had to drive around stalled cars and trucks. And bodies. Literally hundreds of bodies. They were everywhere. Flies buzzed around them. They were in various stages of rot. Texas heat can be hell, even in the fall. I wore my mask despite the heat. The camphor was strong, but it helped with the smell. I tried to dodge all the bodies, weaving around like I was on an obstacle course. But sometimes I couldn't avoid them. I ran over a few bodies and I swear I could hear them pop. Pop squish! I almost threw up in my mask, so I turned up my radio to cover the sound. Feral dogs and cats feasted on some of the fresher bodies, fighting amongst themselves for the choicest meats. They turned violent fast when they had no one to feed them. In the original pandemic there had been a few cases where animals had gotten the virus, but it was extremely rare. Animals that were once beloved pets were now ravaging their precious humans as food. What the world had become.

I had just jogged to the right to avoid a dog eating a man's face in the street when I hit the brakes. A white van had driven through the intersection and stopped in front of me, blocking my way. I reached for the gun until I saw the doors open and the doctors in their white protective suits get out.

Doctors! I'm saved! I can get them to help my husband.

"Oh, thank you!" I fairly screamed as I put my car in park and got out, leaving my gun in the passenger seat. "My husband needs help. Please help me."

One of the doctors pulled out something that I thought was a white gun at first, but it turned out to be a forehead thermometer.

"98.6," he told the others in a somewhat awed voice. "She's immune."

"Yes, yes," I chided. "Let's go back and get my husband. You can look me over all you want then."

They hustled me inside the van, and we drove off, leaving my car running in the street.

When we finally stopped, the doors were opened, and I found myself outside a huge building. It wasn't a hospital, but I didn't know what it was.

"Wait, I thought we were going to get my husband first."

One doctor shook his head as he took my arm forcefully. "Sorry. He's terminal. There's nothing we can do for him. But it's okay. You're immune."

"Then I refuse to help you!" I yelled, trying to pull myself away. "Get your damn hands off me!"

Two more doctors grabbed me, and that's when I realized they weren't all doctors. Some were soldiers. As I struggled, they forced me inside the building and locked me in a room with a big glass window. I sat on the single chair next to a tiny table. A hospital bed was behind me. Many people walked up to the window, talking, and pointing at me. They all looked alike in their hazmat suits, like spacemen.

I'd been locked in the room for over six hours when someone finally came in with food and water. Luckily, this room was also equipped with a toilet that I'd already had to use. It had been humiliating to use it with others staring at me through the window.

I was starving. I gulped half the bottle of water down before digging into my food. It was like school cafeteria food, bland and barely warm, but I was hungry, so I ate it all. I had just finished the rest of the bottle of water when I began to feel woozy. Drugged! I looked up at the window and it was completely full of spacemen (as I decided to call them). They all stood perfectly still, watching me like I was an animal at the zoo. I tried to get up from the chair, using the table to brace myself. But it was a flimsy thing and it flipped over as I put too much weight on an edge. I fell to the floor. I heard thumps at the window as all the spacemen hit the window at once, worried that I might hurt myself. The door opened and footsteps rushed in just as I lost consciousness.

When I woke, I was strapped down by my arms and legs onto the bed. An IV was already removing blood from my body slowly, the tubes tracking to a strange-looking machine that hummed. There was another IV in my other arm and I followed the tubes to a large clear plastic box, trying to figure out what was in it.

"Saline and nutrients. Vitamins."

I jumped at the sound of the woman's voice. I twisted my head to see a female doctor behind me. She was in her spaceman suit, but she was close enough so I could see her face. Her dark skin was a stark contrast to the white suit. Her eyes were brown, and she was obviously very tired; huge dark circles surrounded her eyes. They were watery, and she yawned even as I watched. Despite her ragged appearance she was a beautiful lady.

"It's a prototype. It's made so it only needs to be refilled once a day instead of every hour or two like with a traditional IV bag. The bags are larger and heavier, but they reduce the amount of time nurses need to change them out. The bags fit inside the box. The nurses here nicknamed it the 'juice box.' We were about to introduce them to the medical market, but then COVID happened. We created them here, so we have plenty on hand. You also have a catheter installed for your urine. That one has to be replaced every day."

"You know I'd have been happy to let you have a sample of my blood if you had just gone back and got my husband," I said in anger. "Why did you kidnap me?"

"Because we need more than just a sample. We need a continuous source. There are so very few immunes in the world, and we are working twenty-four hours a day to find a cure. It takes more than just one sample from you. It's required to be taken from you gradually but continuously. The "juice box" keep your body running so you can make more blood. It's a small sacrifice to make. It's the entire world that's at stake here."

"I know that," I spat out. "But you could have just asked."

"We couldn't afford the possibility that you would refuse."

She walked around my bed and checked everything attached to me; then she picked up a clipboard and made some notations.

As she opened the door, she turned back to me and said in a soft voice, "We did go back and check. I'm sorry. Your husband is dead."

Then she walked out.

***

The number of spacemen that walk past my window has been drastically reduced. A nurse comes in a couple times a day to check on me, but it's never the same nurse twice. I don't fail to notice their pale faces and hear their barely suppressed coughs. At least they haven't forgotten about me. I've lost track of how long

I've been in here. Days? Weeks? Months? With my hands strapped down, I can't even read a book. Time moves so slowly. They brought in a TV on my second day here and positioned it so I can watch it somewhat comfortably. All it plays is old reruns from the 70's and 80's, as if it's on a loop. There are no commercials or newscasts. I have no idea what's going on in the outside world.

Although the nurses change out the "juice box" daily, they used to come in several times a day to check on me and to make sure all the equipment was working fine. After a time, they just started coming once a day to change out the "juice box" and the urine bag. Even though the blood machine will hold three days' worth, they collect it anyway. The first time more than twenty-four hours went by without a visit I freaked. My "juice box" was out and I didn't know what would happen to me. When someone finally did show up, she refilled the "juice box" but removed the urine bag completely. The end of the tube that snakes from my bladder now just hangs into a large plastic tub sitting on the ground. The stench of my own urine nauseates me. This was days ago. I think. Maybe a week or two? Going two days without an IV has become more common. I suppose I can live without it for a day, but what happens if they take longer?

***

No one walks past my window anymore. I don't think there are any nurses left, or doctors either. I think they are all dead.

"Hellooo!"

The only response is the TV, which has restarted its loop of old shows. Again. I have all these memorized by now.

"Please, someone, come help me!"

I hear a noise outside my door. A spaceman peeks in the window and waves to me before bending over in a coughing fit. I can see this person fiddling with the keypad to open my door. I pray that they have the code. With a loud click the door opens.

I am saved.

***

My dream dissolves in a rush and I jerk myself awake. I begin crying again when I realize I'm still here.

The dream was that I was freed.

I'm still here, but now everyone is dead. I'm still strapped to the bed, and the IV is still sucking my blood like a vampire. The young woman? She did manage to get my door open, and the chair is holding the door open. But she collapsed to the floor right next to it and died. I've yelled myself hoarse calling for help. There's no one here to answer me. The TV is still playing its golden oldies. I recognize the show; knowing the schedule, it will be cheesy sitcoms for the next two days. I'm probably going to die with a laugh track in the background.

I constantly check my "juice box," hoping it will magically fill up. I wonder how long I can survive now it's runs dry. It's been three days now. What does a dry IV do to a person?

No fluids coming in, and blood going out. What will get me first? Dehydration or blood loss?

I briefly wonder if any other immunes are going through the same thing; then I realize I don't care. It doesn't really matter anymore. The world is dead. It's over. My blood couldn't save it. I couldn't save anyone. Not even myself.

ZÕKYÕ

Nigel Anthony Sellars

The three cruiser-boys were out of cash, out of booze, out of cigarettes, out of weed, and out of work—the latter thanks to the mutated coronavirus. The trio had not changed their gang-color clothes for days. Their disposable blue and silver jackets and trousers of rice paper, cotton fibers, and synthetics reeked of sweat, stale tobacco smoke, and low quality liquor as well as greasy street food. Spots of fresh and dried blood were hidden by the blue-colored areas but stood out as dark spots in the silvery portions. Only their face masks were new, and those were already two days old, close to their expiration dates.

Teddy, the leader, had a harsh, scarred face—the product of the mutated coronavirus, parental abuse, and too many fights to prove both his manhood and the fact that he was the top bully in the neighborhood. Now the scars gave him a menacing, and not particularly human, appearance. The mutated coronavirus had caused the white cast in his left eye and left him blind on that side, but somehow he still knew if someone was approaching from behind on that side. His right eye, his "good" eye, if you could call it that, burned with a malevolence from the depths of hell. All of that scared people away and made the rest of the cruiser-boy *bōsōzoku* unwilling to cross Teddy on anything. In fact, most violent gangs preferred not to upset Teddy with even the smallest of trifles.

"We need money," Teddy said. "All I got in my pockets are tokens for parking or car washes. And I don't even have a car to park or wash."

Tiger, whose striped facial tattoos gave him his name, was trying to make a cigarette by stuffing tobacco scavenged from disposed cigarette butts into the wrapper from a drinking straw, which served as the cigarette paper. He lit his jerry-rigged smoke, inhaled, and started coughing. "Man, that's bad stuff."

"Maybe if you didn't inhale like you were sucking cock it wouldn't be so bad," said the third cruiser-boy. His name was Clocker, a name which came from the scars on his forehead, which resembled the hands of a clock set at 4:00 pm. He'd gotten the scars as a child when the mutated coronavirus damaged his mother's brain. It gave her a vision of Doomsday, so she drew on the boy's head with a wood-burning tool.

"Watashi opera daishiki!" Tiger said.

"I know you like to suck cock, Tiger, you *kama,*" Clocker snapped. "Plus, you like it up the ass, too"

"*Kuso demo due,* Clocker!" Tiger said. "And don't forget I've seen you spit roasted on the *chinpoko* of two sumo wrestlers."

"At least I don't swallow," Clocker snapped.

"*Kuso kurae,* Clocker!" Tiger replied.

"I wouldn't eat your shit even if it tasted like caviar," Clocker responded.

"*Chikushō,*" Teddy said. "Shut up, you two."

More like sycophants than secondary or junior bullies, Tiger and Clocker were intimately connected to each other and to Teddy. In fact, Tiger and Clocker were Teddy's bitches. It wasn't a gay thing. It was not about lust or pleasure but about power and hierarchy.

Teddy was top, and, as bottoms, Clocker's and Tiger's sexual subservience confirmed his rule. To be dominated directly and controlled personally by Teddy, however, gave Tiger and Clocker serious status among all the other cruiser-boys of the city.

Teddy reached into the pocket of his jacket and removed a clear plastic bag containing a blood-stained folded oil rag bulging with a number of odd, thin objects about the size and shape of gherkin pickles. Teddy unfolded the cloth and counted its contents.

'How many we got?" Tiger asked.

"Ten," said Teddy. "But Raoul won't take less than a dozen, so we need at least two more."

"So?"

"So, we go looking for some old *otaku* to jackroll." Fingering old persons was the best. Generational warfare was profitable. While the cruiser-boys weren't licensed to cull, they knew people who *were* licensed, people who'd pay you for each little finger from an elderly person you brought in. But they knew you needed at least a dozen, or Raoul wouldn't give you the time of day. Sure, it wasn't near what the licensed hunters got, but you still got something, and getting a license was too hard. Besides, they thought it was fun to kill people. Hell, hadn't the American President said *otaku* should die and help the world economy? Therefore, it was a "civic" duty to cull the elderly population, Teddy lied to himself.

The only danger was from Harvesters and Resurrectionists. They were always looking for young people. Fresh organs were always desirable and highly priced, but Teddy knew solo Harvesters and Resurrectionists rarely came to this side of the city. Anyway, they were less likely to attack groups.

As if on cue, an old man came toward them. He was well-dressed and even wore an old-style hat covering a full head of hair. He also had a respirator mask on his face to keep out the mutated coronavirus. The man moved a bit slowly, but he walked and did not shuffle, and he used a walking stick. The walking stick had a heavy handle.

The three cruiser-boys surrounded and moved in on the man, pushing him back up against the wall of a building. "Give over, *rōjin*," Teddy said. "Give us your money or we'll kill you."

"And take my right pinkie, of course," the old man said. "I can guess you are not licensed."

"Give us your money, *kusojijii*!"

The old man stared at them. "I may be a *rōjin*, but to this old man, you don't look that big. I am Col. Kenji Yamato, formerly of the special unit of the Defense Forces. I should warn you I'm a *Zōkyō*."

"What the fuck is a *Zōkyō*?" Tiger asked.

"Ah, young fool, you don't know your history." Col. Yamato sized up the cruiser-boys. "I fought in the Zaibatsu wars and survived four outbreaks of the mutated coronavirus. That's because I am a *Zōkyō*. My muscles are augmented with carbon fiber, and my nerves are cyber-enhanced. I'm immune to all strains of the coronavirus. I've fought hand-to-hand with other *Zōkyō*. American, Russian, Chinese, Indian. You don't scare me one bit."

Tiger laughed.

With blinding speed, the old man swung the heavy, weighted end of his walking stick right into Tiger's throat, crushing the teen's Adam's apple and trachea. Tiger gagged, gasped for air, then coughed up frothy blood as he collapsed. He gurgled for a moment, then was still.

Clocker pulled out a knife from his jacket, but Yamato had grabbed the handle of his walking stick and pulled the weighted end to reveal a thin sword blade. The sword flashed like lightning and slashed Clocker's throat. Arterial spray went everywhere as the young man fell forward. He was dead before he hit the sidewalk, the blood filling the cracks in the concrete before spilling into the gutter and flowing down the storm drain.

Teddy, stunned at the fate of his minions, reached for the gun inside his jacket, but the old man was quicker. The gun clattered as it hit to the sidewalk, the fingers of Teddy's severed left hand still wrapped around the grips. Teddy screamed and grabbed at the bleeding stump where his hand had been.

"A gun?" Yamato said scornfully. "Being able to move your finger on a trigger is no skill. You impress no one. You, young fool, are neither honorable nor courageous."

Teddy never felt the sword blade penetrating his chest, slipping between his ribs and piercing his heart. He fell backwards, landing face up. Teddy blinked once, then again, and then stared skyward, never to blink again.

Yamato waited a moment to catch his breath before he lifted each boy's right hand by the pinky and cut off the digit with a single flick of his sword. He carefully wrapped the fingers in a handkerchief and put them in a plastic storage bag along with nearly a dozen other pinkies he'd collected from other young members of *bōsōzoku*. He put the bag in his coat pocket, picked up the scabbard part of his walking stick, wiped the sword blade clean on the boys' paper clothes, then slid it back into the scabbard.

"Not a bad haul for the day," he thought. He removed his cellphone from inside his coat and dialed. He turned on the blood analyzer and put a drop of blood from each digit onto rice paper-covered probes. Each proved clear of the mutated coronavirus, although one boy—the older one, with the scarred face—tested positive for antibodies, which was actually a benefit. Few young people had viable antibodies against the latest mutations.

He dialed a number he'd dial a hundred times before.

"Bounty hunter hotline," said a voice on the other end.

He identified himself: "I am Col. Kenji Yamato, formerly of the special division of the Defense Forces." He gave his identification number and code name.

"How can I help you, Colonel Yamato?" the voice asked. Yamato was a little disappointed that the operator did not immediately recognize who he was.

"I've have just harvested three young donors, and would like to request a Resurrection Wagon before it's too late," he said. "They have been dead less than five minutes."

"Do you know anything about the donors?"

"Three cruiser boys, late teens, *bōsōzoku* unknown, but their gang colors are blue and gray," he replied. "I suspect they are illegal hunters, as they have no licenses on their bodies, and one carried an oil cloth wrapped around nearly a dozen freshly severed pinkies."

"Please enter their fingerprints."

He rolled the pinkies across the phone screen as he had thousands of other people whose fingerprints he had taken when he was a police officer.

"Thank you," said the voice on the other end. "We have identified the attackers as persons of interest connected to a Mr. Raoul whom we suspect of buying severed fingers at a low price from unlicensed individuals and then cashing them in for the bounty."

Ah, yes, Yamato thought. Mr. Raoul, who lacked the ethics and honor one expected even from a Yakuza. Naturally, cruiser boys admired criminals like Raoul, who provided drugs, alcohol, and comfort women to little things like them.

The Resurrectionists' van was on the scene in under a minute. As the Resurrectionists exited the vehicle, Yamato held up his mobile phone to show the chief Resurrectionist his hunting license.

"You're Col. Kenji Yamato?" the crew chief said, almost in awe. "I've always wanted to meet you. You provided the donor whose heart saved my brother's life. I can never thank you enough!"

The harvesting crew came out with body bags and tools to put the dead on ice. In the van, the men would use trocars to replace the boys' blood with chilled saline solution and other compounds. Time was wasting, and delays would make the boys' organs useless for transplant. The Resurrectionists had the bodies bagged and instantly chilled. They even picked up Teddy's severed hand and cooled it. The boys' organs would be transplanted within the hour.

Yamato worried about the chest wound he had given the leader, fearing it might make the heart useless for transplant. Sometimes he forgot how powerful his carbon-fiber augmented muscles and cyber-enhanced nervous stem made him. He asked one of the Resurrectionists.

"Oh, no, sir, not a problem," the Resurrectionist said. "We have some new techniques for repairing damaged organs. Too bad we can't do that to the ones people are born with. Then again, if we could, I'd be out of a job."

"So would I," Yamato said. "So would I."

After the Resurrectionists left, Yamato put the oil cloth containing the ten fingers that the boys had severed into a plastic bag At least this way those who the boys had killed could be identified. He'd donate the bounties to the victims' families. That was the least he could do.

Perhaps eventually the cruiser-boys would learn to respect their elders, who had much to teach them, Yamato told himself. Youth was wasted on the young, the colonel thought, and so too, sadly, was wisdom.

LADY FLORA IASO: PSYCHIC HEALER

Anna Lindwasser

"Flora Iaso Woodbury, get in here!"

Ever since my mom started doing psychic healing sessions over Zoom, she's been annoying the hell out of me.

Today, she's been shut up in the only room with air conditioning for like seven hours, screaming about how she can cure and prevent the coronavirus as long as you send enough money to her PayPal. Yesterday she made me skip my afternoon online classes so that I could design a banner for her website, and then spend the whole evening fixing code that she had broken.

"What?" I ask, leaning against the frame.

"I need you to make lunch. A grilled chicken salad for me, and macaroni and cheese with a side of broccoli for your brother. You can make whatever you want for yourself, but I recommend you choose the salad." She eyes my stomach disapprovingly.

"I have to be on Zoom for math class in thirty minutes," I say, crossing my arms over my middle while imagining tossing her into the Atlantic ocean and having her devoured by sharks.

"I know that," she scoffs, tossing back her thick braid of graying hair. "Don't you think I know my own daughter's schedule? That's why I'm asking for something that will take less than thirty minutes to make."

It won't take thirty minutes, something she'd know if she ever actually cooked instead of making me do everything. I'm not worried about missing math - I wasn't planning on doing anything except sign in anyway. But if I'm on lunch duty, I'll be late for my Twitch stream start time.

Right now I'm streaming Micro-Love, a dating sim where you're supposed to woo anthropomorphized versions of diseases. I just downloaded the DLC for Miss Corona's younger sister, Covida, who's based on the COVID-19 mutation that's been keeping everybody inside for the past year, COVID-24. It's not easy to actually get the DLC since it was a limited release, which means I can count on a decent donation stream from people who want to watch her in action.

I announced my start time on Twitter, and my audience is going to be pissed if I'm late.

Staring at the ceiling and breathing in through my nose, I say, "I'll make mac and cheese for everybody and do the salad for dinner. I can't make two meals in half an hour and still get my school work done."

"Fine, do what you want. But make sure you make it fresh – the boxed stuff is full of toxins."

"Right, because it's totally possible to make macaroni and cheese from scratch in less than thirty minutes."

"Don't take that tone with me, young lady!" She stands up, the blocky wooden jewelry on her neck banging together. I duck out of the room and sprint towards the kitchen. Not knowing whether she's going to follow me screeching about my attitude or stay in her room and do her job, I run to the kitchen and start boiling water for our toxic lunch.

Mom doesn't show up, so I flit between making the meal and helping my 12-year-old brother Cyrus through an essay on the recession caused by the first wave of the virus. I'm trying to persuade him that the sentence "Many businesses shut down in order to avoid indangering the population" would be dramatically improved if he changed the spelling of "indangering" to "endangering."

Cyrus isn't listening. Instead, he displays his lack of interest by pressing his cheek into the kitchen table and whining, "I don't care!" which makes me want to punch him in the head.

What he says next makes me want to punch him even harder.

He says, "I'll send Leland Battista a link to Mom's website."

Leland Battista is so hot that boiling water feels cool by comparison. He's so hot that he's singularly responsible for last year's heat wave. I first met him playing talking birds in our 6th grade musical. We sang a song about how pumped we were to eat birdseed, and he held my hands for two minutes and twenty seconds of it – twenty seconds more than our drama teacher said that he had to. In 9th grade, he intentionally sat next to me in ELA, and I'm 67% sure it wasn't just because that seat was the only available one.

We're friends on Twitter and Instagram, but ever since schools shut down for the fourth time in 11th grade, we've only interacted online. I don't mind him knowing about my online presence, but I cannot fathom anything more embarrassing than him seeing my mom claiming to be Madame Aurelia, the reincarnation of the Greek god of medicine, Asklepios. Considering the fact that he knows her as Maggie Woodbury, former lunch lady at our elementary school, he'd definitely die laughing over that one.

"You do that and I'll head-butt you into the sun," I say, ladling his lunch into a bowl. "Anyway, you're on your own. I have math class."

Cyrus sticks out his tongue. I zip into Mom's room with her meal, then bolt to my bedroom – just in time to get ready for my stream.

I don't have a desk, so my only real option is to stream from my bed. I stole a few of my mom's zodiac-print curtains to hang up as a backdrop. That plus a couple of anime posters is good enough for the time being. As for my appearance, I'm lucky. I'm supposed to plug my best friend's Redbubble shop, so all I have to do is throw on the Plague Doctor t-shirt she mailed me last week – well, that and touch up my purple lipstick and wingtip eyeliner. Not my most inspired look, but it should be good enough to keep the tips flowing.

"What's up, Flowers with Powers!" I say, pasting a big smile on my face. "For those who don't know, that's what I call my fans. Today we're playing Micro-Love and seeing if we can make Covida-chan fall in love with us! As usual, I'll be making dialog choices based on your requests, so keep those comments coming!"

As I activate the Covida-chan route by de-equipping my face mask and talking to the coughing girl in the library, a flood of comments pour in. Most have something to do with the game: when Covida-chan greets me they either want me to compliment her sweet Lolita dress or express fear of catching the virus.

Some have nothing to do with the game: my hairdo is amazing considering that salons are closed, they want to know how long until my 18th birthday, whatever. I usually try to reply to the ones that aren't creepy and don't break up the flow of the stream – audience engagement is crucial if you want to get those donations flowing.

That's how I end up seeing a comment from somebody called happyJJ5k. The comment reads:

ur madame aurelia's daughter, right?

At times like this, I wish I were a cat. Then I could zoom through the house, screaming and breaking everything in sight, and everybody else would just have to deal with it. But since I'm a human being, I just have to keep my facial expression peppy so that nobody else on the stream notices my inner turmoil.

Before I can think of a reply, happyJJ5k continues.

i tried to book an appointment with her, but all the slots are full. i'm desperate - can you help me?

I'm so embarrassed I can barely breathe, but I type back that they should shoot me a DM and we'll talk after the stream. If they're one of my mother's clients, I can't just ignore them.

After I wrap up the stream by persuading Covida-chan to give me her phone number, I check my inbox and find a message from happyJJ5k. It says:

hi flora,

sorry for contacting you out of nowhere like this. like i said in the chat, i'm trying to get an appointment with your mother, but i can't. i have the virus, so i really need it.

i was wondering if you also have her gift, and if you could perform a healing if so. i will be happy to pay your mother's usual rate.

thanks,

melody/happyJJ5k

I lean backwards in my seat, grinding my knees into my desk and chewing my lower lip.

My mother would kill me if I took business away from her – but she'd kill me double if I let a potential client walk away unhappy. I've watched her do her sessions enough times that I could probably pull one off – but is it really fair to tell someone with diagnosed COVID that I can cure them? Shouldn't they go see a real doctor?

When she's not insisting that she actually can heal people with her psychic powers, my mom says, "There's no cure for COVID, so all we can do is harness the placebo effect to help people." I don't know if that's true, or just how she justifies it, but it sure does sound attractive.

I want $200 for ten minutes of work, and I don't want to feel guilty about it. I write back:

Hi Melody,

I'm so sorry that you couldn't get an appointment with my mother. She's doing her best to take care of her clients, but the demand has skyrocketed since the latest COVID-24 outbreak.

I HAVE been blessed with her gift, and I'd be thrilled to help set you on the path to healing.

Please send a payment of $200 to my PayPal. Once processed, I'll send you a link to a Zoom meeting, where we'll perform our virtual healing.

Be well,

Lady Flora Iaso

Within minutes, I get an email from PayPal confirming that Melody sent the money. No backing out now.

***

Melody is a thirty-something with sunken amber eyes. She's wearing a neon color-block tee-shirt and black yoga pants. She apologizes in advance if her children disrupt things: "They should be distracted by the movie I put on, but they might need something."

"It must be so hard to take care of children right now," I say, clutching the folds of the purple robe that I stole from my mother's closet.

"It's hard to take care of them safely," she admits. "Especially the two-year-old – she doesn't understand the concept of personal space yet. Besides, I'm just so tired…"

"Of course," I say, furrowing my brow in what I hope looks like sympathy, not guilt. Am I really going to tell this lady she's cured and let her pass on COVID-24 to their kids?

Yes, yes I am. It's not my fault that she's stupid enough to fall for such an obvious ruse, and it's not like I gave her the virus. She's got kids in the house and she's not even wearing a freaking mask, so she's probably one of those anti-mask weirdos who cough on other people at the grocery store. Besides, if I refuse to do this, she'll just hire somebody else. I'm not doing anything wrong.

"As you may have already heard from my mother, I am the reincarnation of Iaso, the Greek goddess of cures, remedies, and modes of healing. I have the power to heal a wide range of ailments, including all forms of the coronavirus."

I pause for a moment, scanning my brain for my mother's script. I've heard her say it like a thousand times, but it's hard to keep bullshit in your head no matter how many times you've heard it.

Then again, it's bullshit. Who cares if I flub a few details?

"As you know, the virus isn't actually a physical condition – it's a spiritual one. That means that I won't be suggesting any kind of medication, and it can be done long-distance." I lean forward on my elbows, then straighten back up and try to look dignified.

"Our perception of time and space is an illusion. By altering my brain waves to the theta state, I'm able to transcend our understanding of quantum reality and send waves of healing energy directly to you."

She nods along like what I'm saying has any meaning whatsoever. I tell her to close her eyes and open her third eye to prepare to receive healing energy. I forgot what song my mom always puts on when she does this, so I throw on lo-fi hip hop radio beats to relax/study to and hope it does the job. I roll my neck and try to copy the low humming noise my mom makes, and then mumble some shit that vaguely sounds like what a YouTube video told me was Ancient Greek.

Melody is blissed out on my bullshit. I've never seen a smile that wide on anybody, not even my own face when I pretended Leland was asking me to marry him and I practiced my acceptance in the mirror.

I don't know when I'm supposed to stop, but she makes it clear by opening her eyes.

She says, "Thank you so much, Lady Flora. I feel so much better already."

Her eyes look every bit as bloodshot and lifeless as they did before the start of the call, and her breath sounds just as labored. If anything, she looks more exhausted, not less.

Is she lying to me because she wants to lull me into a false sense of security before she opens up a PayPal dispute?

Does she really think that I did something?

Are my mother's methods the real deal? Is she psychic? Am I psychic? Did I actually just heal Melody?

Melody's daughter demands apple juice from the next room, prompting her to say goodbye and end the call. I'm left with a blank screen and the sound of my own heartbeat slamming in my ears.

***

The comments I'm getting are different today.

There's plenty of the usual stuff: people chiming in on whether or not I should tell Covida-chan she's a bad girl for spreading an epidemic, people asking me to describe the texture and shape of my nipples, people arguing with each other about some anime I've never seen. But there's also a massive uptick of people talking about Lady Flora Iaso and her healing powers.

Melody has been talking me up on Twitter – apparently she got like a million followers on the strength of a one-time appearance on a reality dating show.

She says I'm even better than my mother is, and cheaper too. The comments aren't just on my stream, either – my Twitter DMs have been decidedly slided into. At least fifteen people are asking for COVID healing, and there are more people than I can count asking if I can heal other things too: everything from diabetes and leukemia to male pattern baldness and particularly persistent colds.

These messages are making me nauseous, but I can't tell if it's the kind of nausea you get because you're having fun on a roller coaster or the kind you get because you ate bad clam chowder. Should I be excited about this attention, or terrified?

My brain isn't sure what to think, but my fingers are. I set up healing appointments with everyone who asks, and wait for the PayPal money to start rolling in.

***

Within a week I'm working full-time hours at my new business, Lady Flora Iaso: Psychic Healer. I'm still keeping up with my Micro-Love stream, but all my other streams are on temporary hiatus while I focus on this.

I'm still logging into my online classes, but I'm not paying attention or participating at all – instead I have my laptop camera and microphone off and the teacher muted while I take calls from clients on my cell phone. I wish I could focus on Ms. Jiminez's talk about Jay Gatsby's existential emptiness, but I'm too busy telling a 43-year-old soccer mom that once I finish aligning her chakras the coronavirus won't be able to touch her. My grades are tanking but my PayPal account is flush.

Mostly, it feels good. It feels good when the payments drop – especially when they come with a healthy tip. It feels good when my clients praise me. Sometimes it's a simple thank you, sometimes it's people telling me that I saved their lives.

I'm pretty sure I'm not actually doing anything, but it's hard to argue with the results. Maybe the placebo effect really is that powerful. Or maybe I'm actually healing people. After all, I am using my mother's methods. I'd assumed she was lying, but I didn't have any proof of that. Maybe she's the real deal and I inherited her healing prowess. After all, only three or four people actually told me it didn't work, and most of those people chalked it up to their chakras not being properly aligned or a janky Internet connection.

Only one person thinks I'm a scammer - somebody with the screen name defenderoftruth451.

They post a Tweet that says:

Lady Flora Iaso is indangering the safety of her clients by making false claims. If you have COVID-24, you need an actual doctor, not this fraud.

Before I can formulate a response, like fifty people jump to my defense, calling me their angel and their savior.

It feels so much better than my Twitch viewers calling me a stupid bitch who doesn't know anything about video games. As long as I can ignore the gnawing guilt, it feels great.

About a month into this, I'm lying upside-down on the couch, watching TikToks on the new phone that I bought with my healer income. It was expensive, but I'll be able to make back what I spent in a couple of hours, so I don't care.

My view is obscured by my mother, who is hulking over me with bared teeth and eyebrows like slash marks. She grabs my phone out of my hand, so I scrabble upwards and try to take it back.

"This isn't the phone that I bought you," she says, frowning at my Covida-chan phone case. "Where did you get the money for this?" I open my mouth, and she tells me not to answer.

"I know exactly what you've been up to," she hisses. "Your brother told me everything."

Cyrus is standing in the doorway, arms crossed over his madras shirt. He sticks his tongue out at me and I launch off the couch with my fist in the air. Mom grabs my shoulder and pushes me back down.

The word *"indangering"* appears in my mind, and I realize that defenderoftruth451 was almost definitely Cyrus. I shoot him the most venomous glare I can muster.

"What did he tell you?" I ask Mom, still giving Cyrus the stink eye.

"He told me that you started your own business. What's it called? Lady Flora Iaso: Psychic Healer? Sounds a lot like Psychic Healing With Madame Aurelia Asklepios. Would you care to explain why you're stealing clients out from under your own mothers' nose?"

I open my mouth to explain how Melody found me – leaving out the part about the Twitch stream, of course – but before I can speak she snaps that she doesn't want to hear it. "You're going to shut down your silly little business. If anyone asks you for a healing session, you direct them to me. You will give me the profits you stole from me. Do you understand?"

"I shouldn't have to give you the money I already made!"

"You made it by copying my business model and stealing my clients. If you weren't my daughter I'd be suing you for damages. You're getting off easy."

I spend a few minutes scowling and complaining, but I'm actually relieved. The guilt that's been lanyarding my guts is ebbing away. Now I can go back to running my Twitch streams, making less money but not hurting anybody, either.

"Flora," she says, her voice going soft. "You do not have the ability to heal people. I do. By accepting these clients, you're preventing them from getting actual help. You can't misrepresent yourself like that. It's wrong."

"Fine," I say, flopping sideways onto the couch and covering myself with the tarot card print throw blanket. "Just let me keep my new phone. I already sold the old one and I need a phone for school."

I think I hear Cyrus moaning about something, but he's a stupid snitch and I hate him, so I don't bother listening.

***

Leland Battista is starting to post alarming things on Twitter.

dear body: can you pls let me stop coughing for like five minutes i am trying to make lemon basil sorbet and you are being a nuisance.

according to my mom i should not use the punching bag while i have a fever. what, b/c i punched myself in the face?? totally unreasonable.

covid-24 is worse than covid-19 and covid-21 combined. why? because i have covid-24 and i am very important, that's why.

can't think of a joke this just hardcore sucks. if you're still outside not wearing a mask then honestly fuck you.

After a couple seconds spent looking for the tweet where Leland apologizes for his terrible joke, I shoot Leland a text asking if he's okay and if there's anything I can do. There's no reply. This could be because he's busy playing video games or because I'm not cute enough to bother texting back, but it could also be because he's on a ventilator in the hospital. Or dead.

I lightning bolt into my mother's bedroom, leaping onto her bed. I know she's mad, but I also know she's not going to keep holding it against me while the love of my life might be dying of COVID-24.

"Mama, did you hear that Leland's sick???" I shout, scrambling into a cross-legged position.

My mother turns around, face smooshed into the heel of her hand. Her burgundy nail polish is peeling, and her smoky makeup is smudged. Her eyes are swollen as if she's been crying.

"Yes, my darling, I know. I just got off the phone with his mother – she's beside herself, of course."

"How did he even get it? His family's been doing social distancing and wearing masks just like everybody else, right?"

"Yes, but his mother can't exactly repair other people's air conditioners from home. She thinks she might have tracked the virus into the house after work. She blames herself, poor thing."

"You can heal him, though, right?" I lean forward, the heels of my hands digging into her blankets.

"No – the Battistas wouldn't want me to do that. They don't believe in such things."

"But can't you just send your healing energy anyway? They're not going to care that it's hokey if it works."

My mother heaves a sigh that sounds like a sputtering exhaust pipe on the back of a truck. "My methods aren't effective on people who aren't open to them," she says. "A little thief like you ought to know that."

"I'll convince him! I'm good at that! Remember when I tricked Cyrus into thinking he had an evil twin who lived in the subway system?"

"They've been having financial issues lately – they wouldn't be able to afford my fee."

"I'll pay! I'll pay double your fee if I have to!" I grab her arm, squeezing so hard that I leave a white mark. My healer profits might be gone, but I still have what I've been making through Twitch. I'll give away every penny I have if it's for Leland.

Mom jerks her arm away, threads her fingers through her curly graying hair, and sighs again. "You're a lot dumber than you think you are, my girl," she says.

"What do you mean?"

"Don't you think that if I could really heal people, I'd have already done that for Leland? I'm not such a monster that I'd let a child I've known for years suffer for no reason. If I could heal people, we wouldn't have been wasting away in this shithole apartment, now would we?"

Tears bubble in her eyes, and as she swipes them away she swings sideways on her computer chair so that I can't see her face. Voice heavy and heaving she says, "My god, I can't believe I'm raising such a stupid girl. You'll never survive if you can't tell when someone's lying to you."

I leap from the bed, ball my fists, and grit my teeth so that I'm not tempted to straight up bite her. I shout, "Why would I expect my own mother to lie? You told me you had powers for real. I shut down my business and gave you all of my profits because I believed you!"

"You shouldn't have believed me!" Her cheeks are blotchy, her eyes bloodshot. "None of what I said means anything. You can't put your brain in a theta state. You can't heal someone by telling them to open up their third eye, you can't send waves of anything, anywhere, through any method! Why would you think that was possible?"

"Because you're my mother and I trusted you!" I scream.

"Well, let that be a lesson to you, Flora. Don't trust people just because you want to. Use your brain and pay attention so you don't end up getting ripped off like my clients are."

"How am I supposed to be okay with the fact that my own mother is intentionally scamming people?" I want to be yelling at her, but it feels like there's something stuck in my throat. My eyes go wet and prickly with tears.

My mother picks up my hand and tries to thread her fingers through mine. I snatch them away and tell her not to touch me.

Scowling, she says, "You're demonizing me when you did exactly the same thing. How do you think I've been supporting you and your brother all this time?"

She grabs my hand again, squeezing hard this time. "Do you think it's been easy for me to make a living through years of pandemics, with no help from anyone else? Or did you not realize that because you don't think about anybody but yourself?"

"I do think about other people – you're the one telling thousands of people you can heal them when you know that you can't!"

One slap from my mother and I'm staggering backwards onto her bed. I reach up and grab my throbbing face. Her eyes are wide, her burgundy lips curled into a snarl.

"You're a hypocrite," she says, flexing her fingers. "You did exactly the same thing I did, and then convinced yourself that you were actually helping people. You wanted money, just like me. The only difference is that while I'm using the money to keep a roof over your head, you're using it to buy yourself luxuries."

"A cell phone isn't a luxury! I need it to go to school, or did you forget that I'm trying to take online classes while also raising your son and making your meals?"

"You're not even going to your classes! I don't know what you're spending all your free time on, but if you were at your classes then your teachers wouldn't be nagging me all the time while I'm trying to work!"

"That's not even the point! The point is that you're a con artist and you raised me, so it's your fault that I'm a con artist too!"

My neck is bathed in cold sweat, and my heart is thrumming in my chest. I don't care about being a con artist, not right now. What I care about is Leland. "Mom," I choke. "Is he going to die?"

"He might," Mom says, reaching for my hand again. This time, I don't stop her. I want comfort, even if it's coming from a liar. "Listen, Flora, we have to keep peoples' spirits up. After the first vaccine failed and COVID-19 evolved into COVID-24, we haven't had any hope whatsoever. People want to believe that there's a solution. I'm just giving people hope, that's all."

"But Mama, if people think they're cured they'll go and spread it to other people, won't they? Or they won't go to the doctor when a doctor could help them."

"Half of these people are terrified that the government is going to implant microchips with the mark of the beast in their neck. Do you really think they're wearing masks and seeing actual doctors?" She starts combing my hair with her fingers. “Besides, it’s not like doctors can do anything to help them anyway. ”

“So, should Leland go to the doctor?”

“He’s already been to one – his parents took him the instant he got sick. The doctor wasn’t able to do anything other than diagnose him and give him some medicine to help with his symptoms. They couldn’t cure him, that’s for sure. Nobody can cure this, Flora. You have to understand that.”

“I still think you’re making excuses,” I mumble, leaning into her shoulder and watering it with my tears.

I hate how much I want to believe her excuses. I want to keep making easy money, and I want to do it without any guilt. I want that for my mother, too. But no matter how hard I try to believe her, I can’t do it without my stomach twisting itself into a Möbius strip.

Mom kisses the top of my head and says, “I probably am. But it is what it is.”

***

Cyrus and I haven’t spoken since he ratted me out to Mom.

Usually when he does something to piss me off, he gets uncomfortable with the tension and whines at me until I forgive him. One time he ate all of my chocolate, then sat outside my door making weird gurgling noises for almost an hour until I said I wasn’t angry.

This time, though, he doesn’t seem to care that I’m mad at him. When we pass in the hallway, he averts his eyes. Like that little brat has any right to be disgusted by somebody who makes his lunch and helps him with his stupid homework every day!

This is, of course, my mother’s argument. That I should be grateful for her care, and not worry about her morals. If that isn't good enough for me, then why should it be good enough for him? But does Cyrus even care about my morals, or is he just trying to piss me off?

One day while I'm making curry in the kitchen, Cyrus slinks into the room and sits down at the kitchen table. He props himself up on his knobbly elbows and leers at me. I succeed at ignoring him long enough to chop an onion, but after that I can't take it anymore.

I whirl around with a deep frown and a knife in my hand. I'm not going to do anything with the knife, but I like the drama.

"What can I do for you, Sir Snitch-A-Lot?" I ask, slamming my other hand against the counter. "Want to tell Mom I'm using premade curry paste instead of making it from scratch? Because that's about as far as you're going to get – you aren't going to find any more dirt on me."

"That's what you think this is about?"

"Well, what else could it be? What, are you going to tell me you have some kind of moral objection to my business?" I grab a thick, woody carrot and start peeling it into oblivion. "You're obviously just trying to get back at me for making you do your stupid homework."

As soon as the words leave my mouth, I know they aren't true. Cyrus isn't sticking his tongue out at me, and he isn't whining. His expression is serious: brows furrowed, lips curled into a frown.

"That's not it," he says, ducking his head. "I told Mom what you were doing because I knew she'd stop you. I didn't want you to become the kind of person that she is."

"What kind of person do you think she is?" I put down the peeler, walk over and sit down next to him.

"A liar and a murderer," he says, his voice breaking at the final word. He's taking this quite seriously. "People who go to her instead of doctors stay sick. They spread the coronavirus to other people. Some of those people die. Mom's not tracking any of it, but there's no way it isn't happening."

"Don't you think you're going a little bit too far?" I say. The words feel hollow. I know that he isn't. I know that he's right. People like my mother – and people like me – are spreading the disease. For all I know, a chain reaction caused by one of her clients – or worse, my clients – is the reason that Leland got sick.

Cyrus just looks at me. I put my head on the table and groan. "You're twelve. Why are you smarter than me?"

"Don't be so down on yourself," he says. "It takes brains to run a scam."

"True...but what now? I might have shut down my business, but she's still running hers, and we're still benefiting from it. We probably have to stop her, right?"

"I think so."

"Goddamn it."

He pulls out his phone and shows me the website for the COVID Fraud Hotline.

"We're not going to be able to convince her to stop," he says. "We probably have to report her."

"If we do that, she's going to lose her income at best. At worst, she'll go to jail. How are we going to take care of ourselves if that happens?"

"I don't know, but I think we have to do it anyway."

Damn, I used to think that this kid was a bratty idiot, but he's actually brave as hell. My brain is busy calculating whether or not I can afford to file a report: can I get another good revenue stream going? Enough to support both of us? Cyrus is ready to throw his whole life away to do the right thing.

I have to be on Team Cyrus. I have to be on Team Do The Right Thing. I have to do it for the love of my life, Leland Battista. No matter how much it costs.

Swallowing the bile pooling in my throat, I pick up the phone and dial the number. It rings three times, and a woman with a Southern accent says, "You've reached the COVID Fraud Hotline. How can I help you today?"

"Hi, I'd like to report a business that's claiming to be able to cure the coronavirus using psychic healing. It's called Psychic Healing with Madame Aurelia Asklepios and it's run by a woman named Margaret Woodbury. Yes, I'll hold."

BUSINESS AS USUAL IN THE NEW NORMAL

R. Maureen

The beautiful aqua sky and the finely spun tweets of the early morning birds seemed to mock him.

Everyone in the line seemed suspicious. The businessman shifting from foot to foot, the blonde texting rapidly, the mother and child playing pat-a-cake, and the woman muttering to herself.

Any one of them could be an agent watching him.

Freddy knew he was being followed because he was one of those who had gone off the grid as word of the virus got out. The New World Order never enjoyed it when people like him became aware of their plans.

He smiled as he remembered his ex-wife making fun of him, calling him a 'prepper' as if it was a crazy thing. Even though the Y2K panic fizzled out.

People like him actively prepared for worst-case scenarios by practicing survivalist techniques, including hoarding medicines, water, and, of course, toilet tissue. He was ready for anything, with enough freeze-dried food to sustain him for the next decade.

Freddy would not have left his bunker at all except for the travel ban. Once Martial Law Edict #49867 had been enacted every citizen had to get a new travel access card or be taken in for breaking the ban.

Each news broadcast was filled with images of people being dragged out of their homes, held without cause or warrant. Random checkpoints and equally random searches abounded.

All this was not being done by police officers but, instead, by uniformed soldiers operating out of camouflaged armored vehicles. Perhaps most frightening, as more and more people kept coming down with the virus habeas corpus was suspended. Habeas corpus was the legal term for the right of a person under arrest to be brought before a judge or into a courtroom if they felt they had been unlawfully detained. Freddy found this the most sobering, as the suspension of habeas corpus meant that citizens could be detained with no habeas explanation for why they had been detained, and no recourse to a typical court of law.. He did not like the idea of being tossed into a military holding cell and left there indefinitely under Edict #49867. The card was good for six months, so once this was completed he would not have to endure this again for a while, but until then he hoped that the other people in line would stay on their own X's and that this process would move quickly.

Richard was semiretired from a company that made processors. He had started the business himself right out of college and was use to being in charge. Leaving behind the doubters of the world and hurrying through life had always worked for him, so being in line was painful. He took a deep breath and tried to still himself, acutely aware that all his money could not buy him the travel access card, as the government demanded fingerprints as well as a DNA sample for the database. Hating the vulnerability of being in this line so close to such common people, he fidgeted again in spite of himself.

Stela was sweating. They had been in the outside lot for over an hour and thus far had only moved ahead one X each. She knew the drill because the week before she had been in a line for an update on her food card and three days after that the housing aid committee had demanded she come in to address the fact that she had not reported that she owned a dog. She had spent hours trying to explain that the dog did not belong to her and that she had just fed a stray. One of her neighbors must have reported her, as there were spies everywhere wanting to get the so called 'citizen's rewards' for turning in radicals. She didn't understand why giving scraps to a stray dog would be an offence, but she certainly wouldn't do it again and risk losing her housing.

At each government visit there was a temperature check. If the person had no fever then they proceeded to another room to fill out forms. After that step there was the wait in an open lot while the paperwork was processed. Lastly each was being taken into an office to video chat with a state worker. Stela, who was overweight, with sagging breasts and a roll of fat that bulged over the elastic waist of her faded denim skirt, was already sweating. It was just past ten, so all the standing made Stela feel like she had been there forever but leaving the area of her X and getting too close to the others in line could net a fine of up to $900.

Jillian saw herself as an Internet influencer, since her blogs had more views every day. This morning she was clad in tight jeans, bright green platforms, and a formfitting lime tank top. The voluptuous and leggy blonde texted herself the details of the people in line so she could blog about this later. She noticed the contrast between the large woman with the shaggy hair haphazardly dyed an improbable shade of fire red (with graying roots inches long) and the dude with a suit that must cost more then what Jillian paid for her car. There was a lady with a kid, and then there was the man at the front of the line. He clearly had issues. Everyone had on a mandatory mask, but he had two masks and a face shield as well as long gloves and something that looked like an over-sized apron. Add that to his camouflage hat, saggy jeans, and mirrored glasses, and he was a bit of a fashion freak-show, but not in a fun way.

After ninety minutes of waiting Tommy shook his head and rubbed his eyes. They were one X square ahead when he saw a small grass-green gecko dart onto the warming parking lot. The miniature reptile moved in mini hops, occasionally pausing to extend his yellow throat sac before dashing forward a few strides and making it to a wall. Missy, Tommy's mother, had spent the last hour promising him ice cream if he was good. Using her most enthusiastic voice she had assured him, but he was only three and a half. He hated being there, he missed going to pre-school, he didn't like wearing the mask, and although he liked to be cuddled in his mother's arms, he wanted to get down.

As his whine grew louder Missy saw the man in the suit that had probably been tailored in Italy turn stiffly. His forehead lines showed a scowling bulldog face and quarterback shoulders. Richard was not tall, but he made up for it by the way he held himself. The blonde on the X behind him stopped texting to roll her eyes at the yelping tot.

"Listen, I know this isn't fun but we will be out of here soon," Missy said.

Tommy spotted the gecko again ,much closer this time ,so he wretched free from his mother's grip and sprinted as fast as he could.

Freddy saw the child dart around him, followed by his mother. At five foot five Missy was not as striking as the blonde or as homely as the older lady in the ragged clothes, but she was appealing, with glossy black hair that waved in ringlets down her back and distinctive brown skin that glimmered in the early sun. As the boy tripped over his feet, Freddy automatically reached to steady him. The boy's mother got close enough to Freddy so he could get a huge whiff of her scent.

Although Missy was married, her life was that of a single mother, as her husband had joined the Navy months before the virus epidemic. He was stationed in Italy, so to make ends meet she had taken a night job cleaning cages at the local animal shelter.

Cats of all kinds were Freddy's kryptonite. The combined smells of multiple cats on her jean jacket added to her strong perfume made him begin to sneeze, so he dropped his grip on the boy. Tommy's feet slipped out from under him, landing him on his bottom, and he began to scream in earnest.

Seeking a story, Jillian swung her phone around and began recording. "I am in line waiting for my travel card and some old man just hit a baby! He is sick - he has the virus."

"Wait... " Freddy began, but his sneezing fit had turned into a cough, so he could not finish.

Stela had seen the looks Freddy had given her before, so she chimed in, "I saw it too - he grabbed him and pushed him. He has been coughing all morning."

Missy saw the guards coming and realized that she was no longer on her X and that her son's mask had slipped off, which meant that in addition to having to pay a fine she could risk losing custody for letting Tommy be without a mask. Suddenly she was crying too, as hard as her son, and she didn't care that people were watching.

Freddy shifted and tried to catch his breath, reaching into his large apron pockets to grab an inhaler.

His gun slipped out into the open. Richard was the first to notice it. They were in Madison County, in a 'stand your ground' state,, so he was always ready..

"He has a gun." Richard croaked, his voice filled with tension as he pulled out his own weapon. It was a .380-caliber semiautomatic loaded with hollow point bullets. If Freddy was surprised, it was not readily apparent. He knew he was the good guy, so he drew his own gun and fired. The first bullet went wild, slicing through the muscles of Stela's left arm. As the blood began to squirt out she toppled gracelessly, landing with a thud.

Shocked that this man had shot an unarmed woman in front of her son, Missy didn't think about the fact that he was armed. Fueled by anger adrenaline, and the sum of months of tension, she whacked him with her son's oversized diaper bag. Freddy's weapon slid to the ground, which gave Richard a chance to fire. The shot cracked the air.

Freddy could feel the burn of the bullet pass though his neck.

Several more security guards yelled for Richard to drop his weapon, and even as he did so he could feel his blood coursing from his chest. Sweat stung his eyes as he began to lose consciousness. Even as he lay dying they pumped in a few more rounds. The second guard's bullet hit Jillian, who had continued videotaping even as the shots were fired.

"Back to your square!" the head of the emergency team said to Missy in a chipped, efficient voice. Sensing the tension, covered in Freddy's blood and surrounded

by the wounded and dying, Tommy put his arm around his mother's neck and held tight. His head went to her shoulders and his grip was growing tighter by the second. The guards again told her to move onto her X. Missy was now struggling to release his grip, which was in her curly hair. The little boy was wailing and his arms were flying about as the first guard moved closer to help and managed to separate Tommy from his mother, but he quickly launched himself back into her arms. Missy tried to explain. "Please, if you stop and give him a little time he will calm down. I won't..." Then she coughed. And with that the guard grabbed the little boy from behind and yanked. Without another word he held the kicking, screaming child in his arms as they marched Missy into the decontamination center
.

The rain came in spurts throughout the night .Cracks of thunder and lightning tapered off into a breezy drizzle. The blood from the mishap of the day before was washed away, so once again it was business as usual in the new normal.

CONTRIBUTORS

Katherine L. E. White is an award winning poet, essayist, and international best selling fiction writer, who goes about having grand adventures with her family and friends, and then writes about them. She often champions the causes of those on the fringes of society in her writing, while pretending to be an urban farmer. She lives in Southern Appalachia with her husband, two children, and several animals. You can reach her at www.brukatpublishing.com/katherinelewhite, on facebook at /authorkatherinelewhite, instagram @katherinelewhite, and twitter at @kle_white

***

Chris Rodriguez has retired from the horrors of conventional life. She now lives on the brink of inspiration in a 100-year-old cottage in Pocatello, Idaho. Her works have appeared in various themed anthologies including Rhetoric Askew, several by Horrified Press/Thirteen O'Clock, Left Hand Publisher's, *Mindscapes Unimagined*, Parabnormal Magazine, and Blunder Woman Productions, *Wrong Turn,* which has recently won Best Audiobook Anthology at the SOVAS Awards. You can find her latest at https://www.chrisrodriguez-onthebrink.com or https://www.amazon.com/author/chrisrodriguez-onthebrink.

***

Veronica Smith is a lover of all things horror. Whether she's reading, writing, or watching; that's what you will find her doing when she isn't at her day job. She treats every day as if it was Halloween and hasn't yet been fired for decorating her office as if it's a haunted house. She's been writing since 2014, when her first short story was published, and works on several projects simultaneously. She lives in Katy with her husband of over thirty years. She's usually found at local events, as well the pie shop, feeding her weekly pie bingo addiction.

viewAuthor.at/VeronicaSmith
https://www.amazon.co.uk/-/e/B014JCZQT4
www.facebook.com/Veronica.Smith.Author
https://twitter.com/Vee_L_Smith

***

Anna Lindwasser is a freelance writer and educator living in Brooklyn, New York. Her work has appeared in publications such as Adelaide Magazine, The Molotov Cocktail, Black Heart Magazine, The Charles Carter, and on Ranker.com. You can find out more about what she's up to at annalindwasser.com and on Twitter @annalindwasser.

***

Rhashaa Price…is a *Chi-Yorkian*, Born in Chicago and grow up in New York City. She has an A.A.S in Elementary Education from Bronx Community College. She has over 25+ years of experience as a teacher, mentor and advocate for children and their families. Rhashaa has 7 children and 9 grandchildren. Currently residing in Fort Wayne, IN, and progressing in her career as a Director in the Youth Worker field. Co(vengeance)19 is her 1st published story.

***

R D Doan has written numerous academic articles as a Physician Assistant for his "day job," but really enjoys writing tales of speculative fiction & horror. His stories have been published in printed horror anthologies and can be found online in eZines as well. When he isn't working or writing, he is most often found hiking the trails in West Michigan with his wife, two sons and dogs.

***

Nigal Anthony Sellars is a published author with three novels, including *Samurai Wind* (Hydra Publications) and *The Gonaynme Weapon* (Montag Press.) I'm also a former print journalist and a college history professor whose works have won awards in both fields.

***

D.L. Russell is an Author/Publisher with several pen names. His work has appeared in magazines and anthologies since 2008. He short story collection *Hell is an Awfully Big City* will be released in 2021 with additional stories.

***

Kahn Brown Jr. spent 10 years in prison for Pimping some of the most beautiful women in Cleveland, OH. While incarcerated, he honed his writing skills by taking a class, with the original intention of just getting out of his cell a little more. Released in 2015, Brown set his site on being published, and after realizing what he learned about writing while in prison, was all crap, he robbed a liquor store to get the money to take a writing class at the local community college. *Text-Door Neighbors* is his 1st published story.

***

Bill B. Peters is a pseudonym for a forty-three year old Tech Writer with a few sales as a Writer of Fiction.

***

Joanna Michal Hoyt lives with her family on a Catholic Worker farm in a town in northern NY which is slightly smaller, and no less kind, than Beulahsville. She spends her days tending goats, gardens, and guests and her evenings reading and writing odd stories. Her short fiction has appeared in publications including Mysterion, Crossed Genres, and Daily Science Fiction. Her novel "Cracked Reflections," about protests, police crackdowns, and polarization during the textile strikes of 1912, will be published by Propertius Press in 2021. Read more at https://joannamichalhoyt.com/

***

Eartha Watts Hicks is the founder of Earthatone Publishing and Earthatone Books. Former director of publications for Cultivating Our Sisterhood International Association (COSIA), she is a NYFA (New York Foundation for the Arts) artist, a member of the

American Society of Composers, Authors and Publishers (ASCAP), and the legendary Harlem Writers Guild. A fiction fellow of the Hurston/Wright Foundation, Center for Black Literature and North Country Institute and Retreat for Writers of Color, Eartha's writings have appeared in several online publications, including Harlem World Magazine, TheUrbanBookSource.com, and Future Executives.org. She leads writing, self-publishing, and publicity workshops for the New York Public Library, The National Writers Union, and The New York City Parks Department.

***

R.Maureen is an activist for the homeless as well as a full time writer.She has lived in a dozen states and moved 18 times in 12 years,she is currently residing in California enduring lockdown with her new daughter in law,son and old dog!

***

David R. Moller was born in 1964, (Liverpool, England) to a difficult birth, David didn't find his voice until his youth. Years of thinking he was nobody and treated as such. Including a period of homelessness in the desperate Thatcher Years
However, he hit the paper papering over the scars. Found understanding and belief through words. He has been published and performed widely from the BBC, The Tate, galleries and pubs and everything in between.
His poems and stories are autobiographical, others topical and several his take on life. You can discover more about him on the below links .

***

Katia Kozar was born in Washington D.C. but considers herself a citizen of the world. A political animal, news junkie, and activist, she has worked remotely since 2010 and considers "home" to be anywhere with an internet connection. Her first novel, Bullet Dance, will be published in 2020.

***

Mary Patterson Thornburg lives in Montana. She's a writer of speculative fiction, including the novels *A Glimmer of Guile* and *The Kura*, published by Uncial Press, and the award-winning "Niam's Tale." Her first collection of stories and novellas is due out soon. Watch the skies!

***

Josh Carson writes plays about yesterday and stories about tomorrow.

Made in the USA
Middletown, DE
29 March 2024

52300333R00137